DEATH--on the wing

Slade whirled around in his saddle as
something from the thicket in back of
him struck his upper cartridge belt a
smashing blow, ripped through his shirt
and thudded on the trail a few yards
distant. Slade jerked both guns and
sprayed the thicket with lead, whipping
from the saddle to the ground in a
flicker of motion.

No sound came from the brush, nor was there
any sign of movement. For minutes the
Ranger remained absolutely motionless,
every nerve strung to hairtrigger alertness,
ready for instant action. Then he heard,
faint with distance, the click of rapid
hoofbeats fading to silence.

Slade let out a disgusted growl. The
hellion had made a getaway. Reloading his
guns, he holstered them and strode to the
object lying on the trail—it was a long,
gaudily feathered, steel-tipped arrow!

WALT SLADE

Greatest of the Texas Rangers

Walt Slade, ace lieutenant of the Texas Rangers, is the man most feared by the owlhoots and dry-gulchers of the old Texas Border. The sight of this tall lawman with the lightning-fast draw astride his great black horse, Shadow, symbolizes defense of the innocent and the end of reckless careers of lawlessness. Follow the action-packed adventures of Walt Slade in this exciting Western series.

A Walt Slade Texas Ranger Western

TEXAS VENGEANCE

BRADFORD SCOTT

WILDSIDE PRESS

TEXAS VENGEANCE, *by Bradford Scott*

This book is fiction. No resemblance is intended between any character herein and any person, living or dead; any such resemblance is purely coincidental.

1

"BONE CANYON?" The old Mexican herder raised his eyes to the lean, bronzed face of the man who sat across the campfire from him. The herder's eyes had widened a little and a shadow darkened them, a shadow that seemed to flow downward across his face which a moment before had been placidly expressionless.

"Bone Canyon," he repeated. "Bone Canyon, *Capitan*, is a place accurst. Rightly it is named, for it is salted blue with bones, and over its dark walls hover ever the spirits of the slain. Bone Canyon was the stronghold of Cocha, the great Apache War Chief, who defied the armed might of the *Estados Unidos* for many years. Cocha lies buried in Bone Canyon, the exact spot of his grave no man knows. The night he was buried, his followers ran their horses up and down the canyon from dusk to dawn, beating out every possible trace of his grave. And ever after, the dark *Indios* of the mountains shunned Bone Canyon as the spiritland of Cocha. Every year the *Indios* went into these mountains to gather *beyotas*—acorns—one of the favorite goods; but in Bone Canyon, though the acorns are plentiful and of fine quality, they go unharvested. Cocha, say the *Indios*, and those who died with him in the last great fight, ride the canyon on moonlight nights, shaking their phantom weapons at phantom foes. *Si, Capitan*, Bone Canyon is haunted."

"Didn't stop folks from opening up mines there," the listener interpolated.

The herder shrugged with Latin eloquence. "The *gringo*," he replied sententiously, "fears nothing, especially when on the quest of treasure. Doubtless you will go there, too *Capitan*, for as all know, El Halcon fears nothing living or dead."

Ranger Walt Slade, named by the *peons* of the Rio Grande river villages El Halcon—The Hawk—smiled, his even teeth flashing white in his bronzed face, the quirkings at the

5

corners of his rather wide mouth somewhat relieving the tinge of fierceness evinced by the prominent hawk nose and the powerful chin and jaw.

"Not so sure about the living," he demurred, "but I never felt there was anything to fear from the dead. Cocha passed on about fifteen years back, I understand, so I don't figure there's much to worry about from him."

"Perhaps not," the herder admitted, "but strange things have happened and are still happening in Bone Canyon, and the country of Bone Canyon."

"You're right about that," Slade returned, thoughtfully.

"Smoke signals are still seen in the hills, although the *Indios* have vanished these many years agone," said the old herder. "Signals from fires lighted, no doubt, by the shade of Cocha and wafted into the air as a warning to those who desecrate his spiritland."

"From what I've heard of him, Cocha doesn't need to light any fires," Slade chuckled. "Judging from all accounts, there should be plenty already lit where he's gone."

The sheep herder permitted himself a smile, but his face quickly grew serious again.

"Which calls to mind the legend that has grown up around the name of Cocha," he observed. "There are those who say that the shade of Cocha still haunts Bone Canyon because he has no place else to go. That the gates of Heaven are closed to him, and that because of his so great wickedness, even *El Diablo* will have naught to do with his soul. So the soul of Cocha walks the earth in great loneliness, seeking peace, and finding none."

"Well, I reckon I'll take a chance on him," Slade smiled.

"Do you ride to Bone Canyon, *Capitan?*"

"Yes, to Pearson, the town they built not far from the mouth of it after the gold strike," Slade replied. "I understand it is quite a pueblo."

"A wild town, *si*," the Mexican replied. The *vaqueros* who work on the ranches of the surrounding country, and they are many, go there, and of course there are the miners, and others lured by the gold that on paydays flows like water."

"Yes, a rip-roaring cowboy-mining town," Slade remarked reflectively. "Plenty going on all the time, I expect; sort of a center for the whole section."

"Strange men go there," said the herder. He glanced around, lowered his voice, although the site of his camp was lonely and it was doubtful if another soul was within twenty miles. "It is said," he added, "that the shade of Cocha appears there at times. A great man and tall; tall, almost, *Capitan*, as yourself."

"Cocha was a big man, then? Apaches are usually on the short side."

"It is said that the mother of Cocha was a white *Señora*, stolen from a village in my country, *Mejico*," observed the herder. "It was said that Cocha was not dark like most Apaches. A little darker than yourself, I would judge. He spoke both Spanish and English fluently as he did his native tongue. And his wife was white also—a captive taken during an Apache raid south of the Rio Grande."

"He was a sort of Apache Quannah Parker, eh?" Slade mused. "Quannah was a Comanche chief, but his mother was white. Maybe I'll meet Cocha in Pearson," he added with a chuckle.

The Mexican crossed himself. "May *El Dios* forbid!" he prayed fervently. "To meet him face to face is death."

Slade eyed the other thoughtfully. The old man undoubtedly believed what he said.

"Somebody is building up a reputation hereabouts, I'd say," he remarked. "Been considerable trouble in the section, hasn't there, Sebastian?"

"Much," the herder replied. "There have been robberies of stages and trains and the stealing of many cattle. Almost in every instance there have been killings. And time on time, Cocha has been seen, wearing his great war bonnet, the feathers of which sweep the ground."

"Organized outlawry, all right," Slade conceded. "But, Sebastian, you can rely on it, there isn't any Cocha. Sitting back somewhere, the chances are, pulling the strings and lining things up and giving the orders, is some nice mild gent who is considered respectable by most of those who know him and who has been using the ghost angle to get folks worked up and on the run and busy looking for something that doesn't exist. It's an old outlaw trick, so old you'd think it wouldn't work, but it does. Even folks who know better will begin to believe such things really exist."

"Doubtless," the Mexican agreed politely, but Slade could see he was not at all convinced.

"Well, we're quite a ways from Bone Canyon, so we won't worry about Cocha and his ghosts tonight," Slade said, "and I'm so sleepy I'm going to have to take a diamond hitch on my eyelids in another minute or two to hold them open."

Ten minutes later both the white-haired old shepherd and the tall, black-haired Texan were rolled up in their blankets and sound asleep.

Daybreak found both awake. Slade had a hot breakfast with the *pastor*. They talked for a while and then El Halcon mounted Shadow, his great black horse, said good-bye to old Sebastian and rode westward toward where their towering crests tipped with the gold of the sunrise, a range of mountains fanged into the blue of the Texas sky. He hitched his double cartridge belts a little higher about his lean waist, the plain black butts of the heavy guns in their carefully worked and oiled cut-out holsters flaring out from his sinewy hips.

Slade lounged gracefully in his comfortable Mexican saddle, and with equal grace he wore the homely garb of the rangeland—overalls, faded blue shirt with a vivid neckerchief looped at the throat, a battered broad-brimmed "J.B." and well scuffed half-boots of softly tanned leather. With a blanket roll strapped behind the saddle and his plumped-out saddle pouches, he looked no different from any chuckline-riding cowhand ready to exchange a day's work of mending fence or digging postholes for three squares and a little tobacco money. The famous silver star set on a silver circle, the honored and feared badge of the Texas Rangers, was tucked away in a cunningly-concealed secret pocket in his broad leather belt.

The rolling rangeland was aglow with mellow light. A little breeze shook down showers of dew gems from the grassheads. Birds sang in the thickets, little streams gleamed like coils of silver. Slade sang softly to himself in his rich, sweet voice as he rode. Shadow slugged his head above the bit and snorted. Both man and horse seemed bursting with lusty life and thoroughly in tune with the beauty of the morning.

For miles the trail flowed westward across almost level prairies; then gradually it began to climb the shoulders of the foothills that were the beginning of the western mountains. As yet, the slopes were long and gentle, with deep grass-grown and wooded hollows between. Finally, on topping a higher rise, Slade pulled Shadow to a halt and gazed across the intervening ridges to where two black and forbidding precipices towered to form the gateway of a canyon that bored into the higher hills.

So great was the height of the cliffs which formed the portals of the gorge, the canyon though wide, more than a mile from wall to wall, was shadowy. It gave the impression of tremendous depth beyond.

"Well, there it is, Bone Canyon," Slade remarked to Shadow. He gazed at a drifting smudge that lay dark against the western sky. That sable smoke cloud must be from the stamp mills of Pearson, the mining and cow town seven miles up the gorge.

Seen from the crest of the rise, the canyon looked all he had been told about it. There was a grimness to that stony gateway that was more than the expected austerity of dark rock and somber growth. It seemed to hint of bloody doings and age-old tragedy.

From where he sat his horse, Slade could see a faint gray streak running past the canyon mouth, which he knew must be the trail to Cooper, the railroad town some twenty miles to the south.

"Well, reckon there's no sense sitting here and wondering what's ahead of us," Slade told the horse. "The best way to find out is to go and find out."

Shadow unscrambled that one, snorted agreement and moved down the long opposite sag towards the depths of a wide hollow from which the trail writhed upward for a full two miles to the crest of the opposite ridge.

A less-traveled trail wound up from the south to join the main track; some twenty yards from the forks it curved around a stand of high brush, its continuance hidden from view. Very likely it ran up from the cattle ranches to the south and east.

They reached the bottom of the hollow without mishap

and continued across its brush-grown floor. From time to time Slade glanced upward toward the ridge knifing the skyline. Suddenly he leaned forward a little, his eyes narrowing with interest.

As if jerked into view by invisible strings, a horseman had appeared over the knife edge of the ridge. For an instant he loomed against the sky, then hurtled downward, driving his mount at breakneck speed.

"Horse, that jigger sure is in a hurry!" Slade exclaimed. "Look at him fog it! He—now what in blazes?"

Over the crest of the ridge four more riders had bulged into view, three hundred yards or more behind the first, who were urging their horses downward with voice and hand. Slade could faintly hear wild whoops as the pursuers skalleyhooted down the sag. Then he heard something else.

A puff of smoke mushroomed from the ranks of the fast-riding four. A moment later the hard, metallic crack of a gun reached Slade's ears. He saw the lone horseman duck, bend low over his horse's neck, cast a glance backward. Another puff spurted up, and again the sound of the report reached Slade's ears an instant later. A whole volley of shots folowed, the smoke rolling backward from the firing horsemen in a thin whitish cloud. But still the man in front, mounted on a shaggy bay, sped on.

Slade watched the uneven contest with concern. He could see that the pursuers were slowly gaining on the fugitive, and it seemed a miracle that he hadn't already been downed. However, a man on a speeding horse is an elusive target, especially for marksmen on likewise racing cayuses. Just the same, it would be only a matter of time. And four against one wasn't exactly sporting.

Of course what he saw could be a sheriff's posse chasing some miscreant, but Slade didn't think so. He decided to horn in. Backing Shadow into the edge of the growth on the right, where he would be all but invisible, he slid his heavy Winchester from where it snugged in the saddle boot under his left thigh and dismounted. He pressed the butt firmly against his shoulder and cuddled his cheek against the stock. His gray eyes glanced carefully along the sights; he had no desire to make a mistake that couldn't be explained, even if it left anybody to explain to.

Smoke spurted from the rifle's muzzle. The report beat

back from the wall of brush. Slade saw the pursuers duck in their saddles, heard their triumphant whoops change to yells of surprise and alarm. He chuckled as he shifted the rifle muzzle the merest trifle.

"Reckon that one came close enough to give them a scare," he told Shadow. "Now to fan one past right in front of them."

The rifle rang loudly again. This time the four horsemen jerked their mounts to a sliding halt. A third bullet caused them to duck wildly. Slade could hear their bellowed curses as they whirled their horses and fled madly back up the slope. He sent two more slugs whining over their heads to speed them on their way, lowered the smoking rifle and waited for the fugitive to put in an appearance through the brush. If he was a fugitive from justice, that little matter would have to be taken care of.

Then without the least preliminary warning, Slade hurled himself sideway and down. From the growth on his left had sounded a sharp snap as an incautious foot came down on a dry and fallen branch.

Even as he hit the ground a gun boomed from the growth and the bullet fanned his face. Amid the brush a man loomed dark and gigantic.

Slade fired from the hip. The man reeled back with a yell of pain, pawing at his blood-streaming right hand. His gun, the lock smashed and broken, thudded to the ground. Slade came to his feet in a lithe ripple of motion, his rifle muzzle lined with the other's breast. His eyes were cold as frosted steel, his face set in granite lines. He shot one swift sideways glance westward along the trail; the drum of fast hoofs was sounding from that direction, but the horseman would not come into view for another moment or two.

Still wringing his bleeding hand, the gunman glared at Slade. Then over his face swept a ludicrous expression of astonishment. His eyes bulged, his mouth sagged open. He did not seem to see the rifle barrel trained on his middle as he took a step forward, halted abruptly at the sharp click of the cocked hammer, and stood staring.

"Heck and blazes!" he swore in a thick voice. "I thought you were a Harlow!"

2

Slade regarded him sternly. "That so?" he returned. "Open season on Harlows hereabouts, even to shooting them in the back?"

"They'd shoot me in the back quick enough if they got the chance," the other replied sullenly. He lifted his head as the drumming of hoofs suddenly loudened and the fleeting rider shot into view.

"That's my brother Arnold foggin' the track," he exclaimed. "Hey, Arn, this way."

Slade took a step backward and a little to one side, swinging his rifle barrel around to also cover the approaching horseman, who held a gun in his hand. "Far enough!" he called.

The rider jerked his mount to a slithering stop and stared open-mouthed at the tableau presented at the edge of the growth.

"Light off, Arn," the man in the brush called. "I made a mistake."

The newcomer, who was little more than a boy in years, had a frank freckled face that suddenly split in a grin.

"Uh-huh, looks like you did," he remarked dryly, his gaze on his brother's blood-dripping fingers.

"I heard this gent throwing lead up the trail and I knew you were up here somewhere," the other explained. "I unforked and slid through the brush. Naturally I figured him to be a Harlow. He ain't."

The boy, who had holstered his gun and slipped to the ground, stared at Slade.

"Say!" he exclaimed, "you must be the feller who saved me from those blasted Harlows! The Harlows were chasing me, Sime," he explained to his brother. "They were gaining on me. Every jump I thought it was curtains for me. Then all of a sudden a gun cracked down here and I heard a bullet screech over my head. I figured then I was surrounded and a goner for sure, but the slug went on and smoked the

12

Harlows. Others came after it and fanned them proper. They turned around and hightailed back up the sag. If it hadn't been for this feller, Sime, they woud have done for me."

His brother wet his lips with his tongue. "G-good God!" he breathed. "And I came nigh onto plugging him!" He turned to Slade, who had lowered his rifle.

"Feller," he said, "there ain't no use for me trying to tell you how sorry I am. Just put yourself in my place and maybe you'll understand. I'm Sime Bowman and this is my brother Arnold. We're in a feuding with the Harlows and they're out to get us."

Slade nodded. "Looked like they were out to get somebody," he admitted. "Just what is it all about?"

"Well, among other things, they call us sheepmen," Sime Bowman replied. He shot Slade a shrewd look. "Reckon that don't stand over well with you, eh, seeing as you have the look of a cowman."

"I have no objection to sheep so long as they are handled properly, and sheepmen have a right to live, same as anybody else," Slade replied quietly as he slipped fresh cartridges into the magazine of his rifle. "Why are the Harlows on the prod against you? Do you let your sheep destroy range?"

"Heck, we don't own no sheep," Sime Bowman said. "We raise cattle, but we have a big herd of Angora goats, and the Harlows, and some other folks, figure goats and sheep are the same and won't listen to reason. Goats don't hurt range."

"That's right," Slade agreed. "Goats don't."

"But you can't make some folks believe it," Bowman repeated. "The Harlows jumped us as soon as we set up in business in this section. Us fellers are newcomers here, you know, been here less than two years, and the Harlows are old-timers—been here all their lives. Also when we fenced our range we bought from the state, that didn't set well with them either. They claim this has always been open range and should stay that way. But we came down from the Panhandle where they've been fencing for quite a while, and we know the advantages of fence."

'You're right again," Slade conceded. "Open range can no longer compete with fenced pastures, as progressive cattlemen everywhere are beginning to learn. A man with a fenced spread has his stock moving to market before the open range man has gotten well started with his round-up and cutting out."

"Well, I wish more folks could see it plain like you can," sighed Bowman. "A while back I had a real row with Wes Harlow in a Pearson saloon; flung him headfirst into a spittoon. He didn't take over kind to being manhandled—reckon it never happened to him before—and swore he'd get even the first chance he got. Night after that somebody tried to drygulch his brother Tom. The Harlows swore us fellers did it, and the row was on proper."

"I see," Slade commented thoughtfully. "Everybody in the section down on you?"

"Nope, I can't say that," Bowman replied. "Lots of folks hereabouts, especially the newer ones, don't take so kind to the Harlows running everything the way they think best. Sort of a difference of opinion, all right. Lots of folks are nice to us and sort of side with us. Just as lots of others side with the Harlows."

"I see," Slade repeated, even more thoughtfully. He did "see" and knew that a very serious situation could develop. Of course, he realized, he was at the moment getting one side of the story, the Bowman side; he would reserve judgment until he had all the facts. Getting which, past experience told him, would very likely not be easy. He strode to where Shadow stood, slipped the rifle back into the saddle boot and from a saddlebag took a roll of bandage and a box of antiseptic ointment.

"Let me have a look at that hand," he told Bowman. "Nothing serious, I see, just a chunk of meat knocked loose, but it should be taken care of." He quickly and skillfully dressed and bandaged the wound.

"Shouldn't give you any trouble now," he said. Stepping back, he looked the Bowman brothers over.

Sime Bowman was a huge man, tall, almost, as El Halcon himself, with wide, thick shoulders and a barrel chest. His eyes were dark and piercing, his hair almost black, his complexion verging on swarthiness. His bearing, Slade thought, was soldierly.

His brother Arnold, in contrast, was slender and slightly built, with a fair skin and merry blue eyes. He returned the Ranger's gaze with interest.

"Golly, but you're a tall feller!" he exclaimed. "Sime is

six-feet-two, but you're even taller. Sime, I betcha he could lick you."

"Well, he' ain't going to get a chance to try, not if I have anything to say about it," the older Bowman returned gruffly. "A sample of his shooting is enough of him to suit me."

"Uh-huh," Sime replied dryly. "I've noticed that sort of luck before; it generally holds."

"Reckon I'm on the right track to Pearson?" Slade deftly changed the subject.

"That's right," Arnold Bowman said. "I was headed for there myself when I ran into the Harlows. They were cutting into the main track from their spread to the north. I decided it might be a good idea to turn around and come back this way."

"Our holding is to the south of the trail," Sime Bowman explained. "The casa is ten miles to the southeast of here. I was heading for Pearson myself when I heard the shooting, as I said before. I had a few chores to do around the house and Arn left before I did. I figured to catch up with him before he reached town."

"With the help of the Harlows, you did," Arn cut in. "And with the help of this feller you found me right side up, instead of with my toes pointing to the sky."

"And I won't forget it," promised Sime. "By the way, feller, I didn't catch your handle."

Slade supplied his name and they shook hands.

"Well, seeing as we're all three headed in the same direction, suppose we get going," Slade suggested.

"Could do worse, I reckon," Sime Bowman agreed. "I'll get my horse—he's back in the brush."

A few minutes later they were riding up the slope to the crest of the ridge.

"Hope the Harlows aren't holed up someplace waiting for us," Arn Bowman observed.

"Not much chance, I'd say," Sime reassured him. "They'll know we're on the lookout for them and there isn't any place much they could hide. The canyon is open and very little brush, and what is ain't over-high and doesn't afford cover for a horse," he explained to Slade. "Besides, there's folks riding in and out most any time. I figure they'd be taking too much of a chance."

Slade nodded, but once again he reserved judgment and was constantly studying the terrain ahead with the eyes of El Halcon, eyes trained by years of riding the lonely and deceptive trails of outlaw land. Not a movement of birds on the wing or of little animals in the brush escaped his gaze.

They topped the ridge and the trail wound steeply downward to the level range. A mile beyond was the dark mouth of the canyon.

As they drew near the gorge, Slade eyed the towering portals. He noted with interest that on the right, several hundred feet up, the face of the cliff was a broad bench thickly grown with tall chaparral. This bench flowed north until it vanished around the curve of the cliff. Below the bench the cliff was absolutely sheer and the bench petered out just before reaching the gorge mouth. Where it veered around, the perpendicular wall of the north was a full three miles distant.

As they drew near the canyon mouth at a brisk trot, Slade studied the lofty bench intently, and again it was the eyes of El Halcon surveying in minutest detail something that was a bit out of the ordinary and had certain possibilities that could prove unpleasant. The canyon itself might be devoid of good hole-up spots, but the bench was ideal for anybody who desired to keep the approach to the canyon mouth under surveillance.

Not that Slade expected the Harlows to be up there. The ledge could not be reached from the canyon mouth, nor for some three miles at the lowest estimate. What was beyond where the bench curved around the cliff face there was no way of telling, but it did not matter as far as the men who had chased Arn Bowman were concerned.

Nevertheless, Slade experienced a disquieting feeling as the canyon mouth drew steadily nearer. The subtle sixth sense that develops in the minds of men who ride down the years with danger as a constant stirrup companion was beginning to make itself heard in a voice that while inaudible was very real. Sometimes it was aroused merely by forbidding circumstance and surroundings, but at others it had warned of invisible peril, and by heeding the warning, Walt Slade had stayed alive.

Arn Bowman, a merry soul, chatted and laughed. Sime, on the contrary, replied in grunts and monosyllables. Slade was mostly silent, his attention divided between what lay ahead and the talk of the brothers, which dealt chiefly with range conditions in the section.

But by the time they were within three hundred yards of the gorge mouth, Slade forgot all about the Bowmans and heard nothing of their talk. Every faculty was concentrated on the ominous bench onto which the morning sunlight was pouring to outline every branch and twig.

"Down!" he suddenly roared. "Down!"

3

THE BOWMANS were evidently men with quick minds and accustomed to danger. The three forms went sideways from the saddles almost as one.

Almost, but not quite. The bulky Sime was just a mite slow unforking and had barely thrown his leg over the hull when the unseen rifle on the bench cracked spitefully. Sime gave a little grunt, threw up his hands and rolled to the ground to lie motionless.

Slade had dismounted in a ripple of motion. Before the echoes of the shot had ceased slamming back and forth between the canyon walls, he had his Winchester out of the boot and was raking the bristle of growth with a stream of lead. The ejection lever of the rifle was a blur of movement and had a cartridge jammed the metal would have splintered like a drink stick.

"Pepper the brush, pepper the brush!" he shouted to Arn, who had drawn his gun.

The crackle of the Colt joined the deeper boom of the Winchester.

"Hold it!" Slade said as Arn began reloading. Crouching behind his horse, he studied the bench for a trace of movement, and could see none. He shoved fresh cartridges into the magazine of his rifle, his eyes never leaving the ragged line of chaparral fringing the cliff face.

"Keep down, and see how your brother is," he told Arn, without turning his head.

Arn knelt beside his stricken brother, tears running down his face. Slade continued to watch the bench.

Nothing moved there. No more shots sounded. Slade's glance traveled along the ledge to the mistily distant bulge that hid its continuance from view. Finally he lowered the rifle and stepped boldly into view. Still nothing happened.

Slade hadn't expected anything would. He studied the bench a moment longer, then turned to the wounded Bowman.

"We either plugged him dead center or he hightailed right after he fired the shot," he remarked apropos of the unseen drygulcher. "How's Sime?"

"I—I reckon he's done for," Arn gulped, pointing to a ragged tear in the back of Sime's shirt.

Slade said nothing but proceeded to shuck off Bowman's shirt to reveal his sinewy back and shoulders. Across the spine, just above the waist line, was a slight furrow which oozed a few drops of blood. Slade probed the wound with sensitive fingers; his face brightened with relief.

"I don't think he's badly hurt," he told Arn. "The slug grazed his backbone—hit him a hard lick. It appears to have slightly paralyzed him and knocked him cold. I believe he'll come out of it in a few minutes. See—his hands are moving already."

A few minutes later, Bowman opened his eyes and stared dazedly about. With Slade's assistance he sat up, pale and shaky, but apparently otherwise little the worse for his experience. He burst into a torrent of profanity directed against the Harlows. Slade said nothing but studied the lofty bench with speculative eyes.

"How far around the bulge before that ledge slopes down to the ground, if it ever does?" he asked suddenly.

"About a mile," Arn answered.

Slade nodded, his eyes thoughtful. He assisted Sime to his feet "How do you feel?" he asked.

"Not so pert," Bowman admitted, adding, "but I've a notion I'll be okay in a little while. Feel sort of numb all over, but the feeling's passing. Another inch and I'd have been a goner, I reckon. Would have busted my backbone all to pieces. Feller, you saved me by letting out that yelp. Otherwise I reckon I'd have gotten it dead center."

"Probably," Slade conceded. "Lucky you moved fast."

"But not quite fast enough," Sime grunted.

"Enough to spoil the hellion's aim as he pulled trigger," Slade remarked.

"How'd you catch on to him?" Sime asked.

"Was sort of giving that bench a once-over and caught the shine of his gun barrel as he shifted it to line sights," Slade explained. He began reloading his rifle. "Will have to buy

shells first thing when I get to town, at the rate I'm going,"
he growled, "almost emptied my belt. This is a hard section
on ammunition."

"I sure hope you didn't waste all those cartridges," Sime
Bowman spat vindictively. "I hope you belly-shot that side-
winder and left him to die sweatin' up there in the brush.
You didn't get a look at him?"

Slade shook his head. "Just the gleam of his gun barrel. I
figure I either got him dead center with the first shot or he
slid off and hightailed right after he threw down on us. I'd
say the latter. He must have seen you fall and figured he'd
done for you, which appears to have been the general idea.
Not much doubt as to whom he was shooting at. No, I didn't
get a look at him. He was a smooth worker, all right, and
must have moved like an Indian. Well, if you're able to fork
your bronc, we might as well be making another try for
town. I've a notion a drink would sit pretty well with you
about now."

"It would," Sime grunted reply, "several of them. If I keep
on losing meat at the rate I've started out today, I'll soon be
able to join a circus as the living skeleton. Golly, but my
back feels sore!"

They mounted and rode on, warily eyeing the bench. Nothing more happened, however, and a few minutes later they
were between the towering walls of the gorge.

As they entered, Slade noted that the trail within the canyon was much broader, deeply rutted and showing other
signs of much travel. A branch, also much used, turned
sharply south, skirting the cliffs. A less clearly defined track
flowed into the north.

"That's the way to the Harlow ranchhouse," Sime Bowman
observed, gesturing with his thumb to the northern branch.
"The other one heads for Cooper and the railroad. Supplies
for the town and the mines come by way of it, and the gold
wagons use it to pack the metal to Cooper."

A few minutes later they met a huge rumbling wagon
pacing down the canyon. It was drawn by six frisky mules
who showed a willingness to climb the side cliffs or do anything else unorthodox if given an opportunity. A bewhiskered
driver was hurling appalling profanity at them but in a jovial
voice.

"Hi-yuh, Bowman!'" he bawled. "Met three of the Harlow

boys about an hour back, fogging it for town. They appeared to be in a mite of a hurry and were cussing like blazes as they went past; something sure had got 'em riled."

"They'll be in more of a hurry if I line sights with them," Sime Bowman replied vindictively.

"Good hunting'l" the driver whooped cheerfully and roared on in a whirl of mule squeals and profanity.

Slade turned his level gray eyes on Sime Bowman's face.

"Latigo the war talk, it doesn't get you anywhere," he advised quietly. "Besides, you haven't any proof it was the Harlows who drygulched you."

"You heard that teamster say he met *three* of them, didn't you?" Bowman countered. "Arn says there were four chased him down the sag. That means one didn't ride to town. I'll bet my last peso the fourth sidewinder was holed up on that bench waiting for us."

"And I'll bet he wasn't," Slade countered in turn.

Bowman stared at him. "What makes you so blasted sure?" he demanded.

"Well, if he was," Slade replied dryly, "he sure smashed a fundamental law of physics all to flinders."

"Now what in blazes do you mean by that?" asked the bewildered rancher. Slade proceed to patiently explain:

"It is an axiom of physics that no two bodies can occupy the same space at the same time. The corollary is that no body can occupy two different spaces at the same time."

Sime Bowman threw out his hands in despair. "Feller, I ain't exactly ignorant—had enough book learnin' to make first sergeant in Uncle Sam's cavalry—but you leave me trailing way behind you. Just what the devil *do* you mean?"

"Remember what the teamster said," Slade answered. "He said he met the Harlows about an hour back, which is what was to be expected when you take into consideration the time they headed back from where they were shooting at Arn. All right. Now Arn told me that bench from which the shot was fired runs for another mile beyond where it curves around the bulge three miles to the north. Which means the fourth Harlow would have had to ride four miles north, climb a steep slant to the bench and then have ridden four more miles of hard going back to where the bench overlooks the canyon mouth in something like thirty minutes or less. So the only explanation of his being up there that I can think of was the rather unusual ability to be in two places at the same time. Understand, now?"

Young Arn giggled. Sime scowled, scratched his bristling black thatch and wagged his head. Then he grinned, showing crooked but very white teeth.

"All down but nine, set 'em up on the other alley!" he chuckled. "Yep, I see it, you're right. He *couldn't* have gotten back in time. Reckon the fourth hellion headed back to their ranch for some reason. Maybe you held a bit low one time and nicked him," he added hopefully.

"I don't think so," Slade smiled, "but it does look like perhaps he headed for home."

"That's what I'd—" Bowman began, then suddenly chopped off whatever he had intended saying. "But say, if it wasn't one of the Harlows, who was it?"

"That you should be able to answer better than I can," Slade returned dryly.

"Well, I can't," Bowman declared. "I don't know of anybody else that bad on the prod against us. As I said, plenty of the old-timers side with the Harlows but we've never had any real trouble with them. It's got me beat."

"I wonder could a Harlow have been holed up there all the time, waiting for us to come along?" suggested Arn.

"Barely possible, but doesn't sound logical," Slade answered. "Did you advertise the fact that you intended to ride to town this morning?" Both Bowmans shook their heads.

"Also, if such a thing had been planned, it doesn't sound reasonable that the other four would chase Arn back away from the drygulcher," Slade added. "And so far as I can see, the meeting betwen Arn and the four Harlows was purely by chance."

"That's right, I'd say," Arn nodded.

"So the theory that a Harlow was holed up on the bench doesn't seem to hold water," Slade summed up.

Sime Bowman again threw out his hands in an expressive gesture and shrugged his thick shoulders.

"Too much for me," he said. "Oh, to heck with it! Let's get to town and that drink in a hurry. Now I *do* need one."

They rode on, Slade's face even more thoughtful than before. If Bowman was correct in his contention that nobody in the section that he knew of, other than the Harlows, had a grudge against him, who was it planned deliberate murder

and came within a hair's breadth of success? Slade was becoming more and more of the opinion that he had arrived in
the section not a bit too soon.

"Yep, I guess you're right, there couldn't have been a
Harlow holed up on that bench," Sime Bowman remarked
presently. He added, his face darkening, "But there's no
doubt about what the Harlows tried to do to Arn on an open
trail. That I *ain't* forgetting."

As they progressed up the canyon, a deep, monotonous
hum became apparent, vibrating the air, echoing back from
the cliffs. It increased to a sonorous pounding and rumbling.
Slade knew it to be the ponderous steel pestles of the stamp
mills doing their steady dance on the gold ore, grinding it
to a watery paste that, in the amalgam pans, would be
treated by the quicksilver process and the metal separated
from the rock that formed the gangue of the vein in which
the gold was found. Big stamps, too. Evidently the deposits
in the sections were good paying ones.

Another half hour of riding and they rounded a turn and
the town lay before them, a huddle of ramshackle buildings
dominated by the gaunt structures that housed the stamps.
The walls of the shacks were raw with the color of freshly
sawn, unpainted boards. There was even a dotting of tents
which accommodated newcomers unable as yet to find more
comfortable dwellings. The rasp of saws and the steady clack
of carpenters' hammers promised that the deficiency would
soon be remedied. It appeared every other building housed
a saloon, gambling house or other places of dubious antecedents. A typical Texas boomtown, growing so fast it
couldn't hold itself.

They passed through the straggling outskirts of the town
and reached the main street. Long hitchracks lined the outer
edges of the board sidewalks. The streets were rutted and
deep with dust. A number of horses were tethered to the
racks and Slade noted that the rigs were usually equipped with
saddle boots from which thrust the stocks of rifles. Gents
evidently made a practice of going heeled in the section.

Directly ahead loomed a rambling false-front that boasted
plate glass windows across which was lettered in gold,
Alhambra Saloon. In front of the swinging doors stood a lanky
old man with a big nickel badge pinned to his vest. He had
a drooping mustache, houn' dog chops, cold blue eyes, and

a sawed-off shotgun cradled in his arm. As they came abreast of him he gestured up the street with the shotgun.

"Keep going," he directed in a harsh voice. "The Harlows are in here and I don't aim to have any gunning."

4

Sime Bowman growled surlily under his breath but did not choose to argue.

"That's Sheriff Jess Cross," he told Slade as they rode on. "He's about moved up here from Cooper, the county seat, of late. Spends most of his time here. He's a cold proposition."

"Looks it," Slade agreed.

"Uh-huh, and he's plumb ready to use that scattergun," Sime added. "A square-shooter or I'm a heap mistaken, but he don't stand for no foolishness. I reckon the Harlows have got their orders to stay indoors till we're out of sight. Well, here's the Ace High, Dirk Hudson's place. We might as well light off here."

They tied their horses at a rack and entered the saloon. Sime Bowman bellowed a greeting to a man standing at the end of the long bar.

"Come a-runnin', Sol!" he shouted. "Want you to know Walt Slade, a prime feller. Slade, shake hands with Sol Bajo, he's Dirk Hudson's head floor man and he's top-hole."

Sol Bajo was a tall man, broad of shoulder, lean of waist. He had a regularly-featured and extremely handsome face. His hair was dark, his eyes a very deep blue. He approached with lithe grace and shook hands with a firm grip, his thin, well-shaped lips forming a pleasant smile.

"Anybody Sime speaks well of is okay with me," he said. "Have a drink on the house."

"Where's Dirk?" Sime Bowman asked as they raised their glasses.

"He's in the back room," Bajo replied in his pleasantly modulated voice. "I'll tell him you're here."

"Sol and Dirk Hudson are about the best friends I've got in this section," Sime Bowman remarked to Slade as the floor man moved away. "Sol's smart—got plenty of book learning. He owns a little horse ranch to the north of our holdings.

25

Works for Dirk most of the nights and some busy days, when he can find the time. A good man on the floor, sees everything, and he gives Dirk a hand with his book work. Dirk is okay, too, and between the two of them they sure run this place right. Games are square, drinks are what you order and they don't stand for any foolishness with the dance-floor girls; insist that they be treated as ladies. They can both be plenty salty if necessary. Everybody respects them both."

Slade nodded. The floor man had that sort of look about him. He pondered Bajo's rather peculiar name. Somehow, it struck a responsive chord of memory and he felt he had heard it before. But just when or where or in what connection he couldn't at the moment recall. He did feel, however, that it was not in any connection detrimental to its owner.

Dirk Hudson, the saloon owner, appeared a little later, a slender, broad-shouldered, elegant man who seemed to move on springs. He wore black, relieved only by the snow of his ruffled shirt front. He was tall as Sol Bajo, but in contrast to the floor man, who was almost on the blonde side, his complexion was dark to swarthiness and his eyes were black, with a piercing look to them. His manner was cordial but reserved, his smile a shadowy movement of his mouth. Slade decided that the chief impression he gave was of steely strength and a capability of emotion that was firmly held in check. Slade also felt that he might have some Spanish or other Latin blood; his eyes and complexion seemed to say so. His greeting was not lacking in warmth and he appeared genuinely fond of Sime Bowman. He conversed pleasantly for a few moments in a low and rather musical voice, ordered a drink on the house and departed to attend to his multitudinous duties. Slade was of the opinion that Dirk Hudson was capable of running a tough saloon in a tough town right up to the hilt and also that in Sol Bajo he had a dependable assistant.

It soon became apparent to Slade that the Bowmans were popular in the Ace High. Several men in cowhand dress greeted them, as did others in the unmistakable garb of miners. Sime Bowman seemed to read his thought.

"As I told you, not all the fellers of the section are bullheaded and cantankerous as the Harlows," he explained. "Some of the cowmen recognize the difference between sheep and goats and act accordingly, but you can't tell the Harlows and their clan anything. They're set in their ways and when they get a notion in their thick heads, it stays there. Of course they've sort of been used to running things in the section. I figure they don't take over-kind to mining here in the canyon. The mines brought in lots of new folks who don't figure the Harlows to be so over-much."

Slade nodded. He had encountered similar situations in the course of his Ranger activities and understood perfectly how old-timers, cattle barons of the open range and accustomed to lording it over their fellows and being looked up to, would resent the arrival of newcomers in the section and react accordingly. Men who followed mine strikes were a hardy lot, naturally independent, and impatient of customs and traditions that tended to slow the wheels of progress. The big ranch owners of cattleland, comfortable on their vast domains and content with the existing order of things, did not take kindly to having that order disrupted. In this section, the Harlows had evidently for many years been a law unto themselves and resented any change that would tend to dispute their rule. Also, Slade had learned from Captain Jim McNelty, when the famous commander of the Border Battalion had dispatched his lieutenant and ace-man on his latest chore, that until a short time before, the section was peaceful. But in the past year, it had been plagued by outlaw activities. The Harlows and those who thought as they did would not unnaturally blame the trouble on the influx of newcomers. Which, in fact, was at the bottom of the trouble and responsible for the conditions Ranger Walt Slade had been sent to rectify. Not knowing just who the malefactors were, the old-timers would be in a temper to whack any head that showed, not stopping to reason that they could be doing an injustice to folks as innocent of wrongdoing as themselves.

Again, Slade did not forget that so far he had still heard only the Bowman side of the story. What the Harlow side was he had yet to find out. Sime Bowman had the look of a hard man, and there was but little doubt that he *was* a hard man, one who would very likely ride roughshod over opposition. The Harlows might be justified in their resentment.

Sime Bowman became more convivial as repeated snorts of redeye warmed him. Slade drank sparingly. Finally he set his empty glass on the bar.

"I think I'll look up a place to stable my horse," he told the Bowmans.

"There's a good place right around the next corner," Sime said. "You can get a room over the stalls, too, if you aim to sleep in town. Arn and me would be mighty pleased to have you ride back to our *casa* and spend the night, if you'd be so minded."

"I believe I'll stay in town tonight," Slade declined the invitation. "I've had enough riding for today, but I may take you up on it, later."

"Offer is open, any time, and all the time," Sime said. "Us fellers are pretty deep in your debt, Slade. If it wasn't for you one or both of us wouldn't be here right now. Coming back here to eat?"

"Expect I will," Slade agreed, after a moment's hesitation. "Yes, chances are I will."

"Okay, we'll wait a while for you."

Slade left the saloon and retrieved Shadow. It got dark early between the high walls of Bone Canyon and the dusk was already sifting down like blue dust from the hilltops. The sun had vanished behind the lofty cliffs and on their crests played strange and glorious fires that reflected from the blazing sunset sky above. The dark eyes of windows had changed to squares and rectangles of ruddy gold. Workers were streaming in from the mines and the town was starting to hum with quickening life.

Slade found the stable with no difficulty and arranged for Shadow's care and a sleeping room for himself, in which he deposited his rifle and riding gear. Then he strolled back to the main street, now inadequately lighted by lanterns hung on poles in the time-honored Western fashion. The feeble glimmer was supplemented by the bars of radiance streaming through windows and over the swinging door of the saloons, so that the main street was comparatively bright and cheerful. He did not pause at the Ace High but continued down the street and turned in at the Alhambra. Sheriff Cross and his shotgun were no longer in evidence.

As Slade entered the saloon a sudden hush fell over the big room. His eyes narrowed slightly and he instantly became watchful as he walked unconcernedly to the bar and ordered a drink. Reflected in the back bar mirror he noted a big bulky man with a lined face, cold blue eyes and tawny hair sprinkled with gray disengage himself from a nearby group.

The big man moved ponderously forward until he was within a yard of Slade. He paused and looked the Ranger up and down.

"My name's Wes Harlow," he announced without preamble.

Slade returned the other's gaze, a hint of amusement in the depths of his cold eyes. A regular old snortin' shorthorn was his diagnosis.

"Glad to know you, Harlow," he acknowledged.

Wes Harlow snorted, his eyes hard on Slade's middle.

"Saw you ride in with the Bowmans," he said.

"Good eyes," Slade commented.

Harlow jerked his gaze upward, then again dropped it to Slade's cartridge belts.

"Two-gun man, eh?" he remarked. "Reckon the Bowmans brought you in to do their fighting for them."

Slade smiled slightly, but neither affirmed nor contradicted the statement. Harlow eyed him truculently.

"Just want to tell you," he growled, "that it'll be a hefty chore to pack, even for—El Halcon!"

There was a stir at the bar as Harlow pronounced the last two words. Men turned from their drinks to stare. Dealers looked up from their cards. Poker players seemed to forget the hands they held. Even the bartenders paused with bottles in their hands to regard, with awe, the almost legendary figure whose exploits, some of them considered questionable by many, were the talk of Texas and the Southwest. The man who, among other things, backed down Wyatt Earp, Doc Holliday and Curly Bill Brocious and ended up making firm friends of the famous peace officer and the notorious outlaws. El Halcon! Who, "If he isn't an owlhoot, he misses being one by the skin of his teeth!" "Outlaw, the devil! He's a square shooter if there ever was one! If he's an outlaw, why doesn't some sheriff throw him in the calaboose?" "Because he's too blasted smart to get caught, that's why. He's killed people, ain't no doubt about that!" "Ever hear of him killing anybody who didn't have a killing coming?" And so on, *ad infinitum!*

Slade's gaze did not waver. He smiled down at Harlow from his great height.

"You figure the Bowmans need somebody to do their fighting for them?" he inquired mildly. "Seems to me, from what

I've heard, that *you* should be in a position to know better."

Wes Harlow stared, seemingly taken aback by Slade's smiling good humor. Doubtless he had expected denial or blustering truculence. He was apparently at a loss how to answer.

"If the Bowmans didn't bring you in, what the devil are you doing in this section?" he finally burst out.

"Where's the jury?" Slade inquired.

"Wh-what?" the cattle baron stuttered, more bewildered than before.

"You see," Slade explained cheerfully, "the last time I had a lot of questions put to me, there was a jury sitting alongside."

Somebody laughed. Wes Harlow flushed darkly. Mechanically his hand dropped to the butt of the heavy gun swinging low on his hip. Slade did not move. He continued to regard Harlow with smiling eyes. Harlow fumbled his fingers together uncertainly, then raised his hand and rasped his stubbly chin.

"Oh, the devil!" he exploded at last. "I reckon swapping words with you is about the same as what I've heard tell swapping lead with you is like; but what I said stands. You'll be packing a hefty chore if you take up with the Bowmans."

He turned and strode back to his companions, two of whom, Slade judged from their resemblance to him, were his brothers.

Slade finished his drink in leisurely fashion and left the saloon, conscious that the eyes of the Harlows followed him through the swinging doors. He chuckled as he strolled back toward the Ace High. There were certain humorous aspects to his encounter with the irrascible old cattle baron. At least from the viewpoint of El Halcon.

In fact, Slade was not at all displeased that Wes Harlow or some associate of the cattleman had recognized him as El Halcon, although he knew it might well involve him in personal danger. For he had found that the dubious reputation built up through his habit of at times working under cover and not divulging his Ranger connections often acted to his advantage. For instance, in the course of an extremely hazardous chore which took him to Arizona, El Halcon's reputation, which preceded him to the silver town of Tombstone, while it came close to embroiling him in trouble with

the famous frontier marshal, Wyatt Earp, had enabled him
to obtain information from Curly Bill Brocious, John Ringo
and others of the notorious Cochise county outlaw gang that
would never have been divulged to a known peace officer. A
similar result might be obtained in Pearson.

What he did hope was that nobody would recognize him
as a Ranger, at least for a while.

Slade was not primarily interested in the row between the
Bowmans and the Harlows, although it would bear watching,
for it could easily erupt into a range war with fatalities on
both sides. The information received by Captain McNelty left
no doubt but that there was an organized outlaw bunch
operating in the section, drawn to it by the gold strike and
the resultant boom in business of all kinds. A bunch the local
authorities appeared powerless to cope with.

It was an old story, familiar enough to the Rangers: a
section that had been comparatively peaceful for years, with
only an occasional flare of violence, some petty cattle stealing
and similar minor lawbreaking to disturb the local peace
officers. Things a sheriff or marshall with a fast gunhand and
a stiff backbone could easily keep under control. Then a
sudden boom of some kind, money pouring in, an influx of
newcomers, conditions changing with bewildering rapidity.
Things to interest outlaws who knew their business. Abruptly
the easy-going sheriff, who very likely was a former cowhand
or storekeeper, was confronted with something completely
beyond the range of his limited experience and which from
lack of training and mental equipment he was totally unfitted
to combat. One glance at Sheriff Cross had convinced Slade
that the old fellow belonged to that category. Should an
occasion for courage and fighting ability arise, he would be
there with whetstones and whiskers, but that was as far as
he went.

Anyhow, somebody, in the idiom of the West, was raising
cain and shoving a chunk under a corner. It was up to Slade
to find out who was doing the "raising," which promised to
be something of a chore. Sheriff Cross would naturally suspect
the newcomers, and probably he was right. But possibly he
was not. The real miscreants might have been in the section
for quite a while. That possibility had to be considered. Slade
was inclined to rule out the Harlows at once, but the Bowmans
were a horse of a different color. Slade gathered that they

had settled in the section some time before the gold strike; but he would have to learn more as to their antecedents before giving them a completley clean bill of health. Which applied to everybody else in the section, for that matter. Right now, so far as he was concerned, everybody was suspect, including the sheriff, he admitted, with another chuckle. He turned in at the Ace High.

The Bowmans were still at the bar and greeted him uproariously and insisted he have another drink, which Slade declined.

"Right now I hanker for something to eat," he told them. "Care to join me?"

"A good notion," Sime agreed. "Feel the need of something to hold this snake juice down."

While they waited for the food to be prepared, Sime glanced around with evident satisfaction. "I like this section," he confided. "Some nice folks hereabouts. Not all like the Harlows. I'm glad I coiled my twine here, even though we have had trouble."

"How did you come to settle here in the first place?" Slade asked.

Bowman chuckled. "I was always curious about the section because my dad used to talk about it," he replied. "And when I pulled out of Uncle Sam's Army—I served ten years—having some money saved up to add to what Dad left, and with Arn growing up enough to be of help, I browsed around a bit and finally decided to buy state land here. Sort of a homing pigeon instinct, I reckon. Dad had talked so much of the section I sort of felt like I belonged here. You see, my dad commanded the cavalry detachment that did for Cocha, the Apache War Chief, and his braves. He used to tell me about the big fight here that finished Cocha. Like to hear about it?"

Slade nodded and Bowman began. As the tale progressed, Slade realized that big Sime knew the art of telling a story well. The grim drama of years gone by seemed to unfold before his eyes as if the actors in it were present.

5

IN THE DEPTHS of Bone Canyon, where the towering walls were replaced by long slopes thickly covered with tall chaparral growth, the War Chief Cocha and his Mangas Apaches made merry. Their last raid, on a wagon train, had been highly successful. Among other things valued by the Indians, the train had provided a number of kegs of whiskey. Secure in their hidden stronghold, the Apaches were consuming great quantities of food and washing it down with the white man's firewater. Cocha, tall, erect, his white blood showing in his lighter coloring and lither figure, stood near the central fire. Nearby sat his blue-eyed Spanish wife, the mother of his son, old before her time, staring somberly into the fire. The braves danced about the fires, sang and shouted. Abruptly, however, Cocha raised his head in an attitude of listening. From around the bend down-canyon welled a rhythmic clicking. Even as Cocha shouted an order, the brassy, ringing note of a bugle blared forth, sounding the charge.

The Indians raced to their ponies, tethered nearby, and mounted in hot haste, gripping their weapons.

Around the bend stormed a blue-clad cavalry troop in the wake of the screaming bugle. Rifles cracked, braves spun from their horses. Others fired wildly or fled up the slopes to the shelter of the thick growth.

Cocha, utterly fearless, imbued with bitter hatred of the whites, rode forward. He flung his rifle to his shoulder, lined sights with the broad breast of the captain riding in front. The rifle cracked, the captain reeled in his saddle, steadied himself and thundered forward. Cocha fired again. Then the heavy cavalry saber flashed up and down. Cocha pitched from his pony's back, his skull cloven, to lie in a bloody heap on the ground.

The troop stormed through the camp, shooting and slashing.

33

The Spanish wife slumped forward onto her face; a chance bullet had caught her squarely between her staring eyes.

The ground was dotted with slain Apaches; but now smoke began spurting from the growth on the slopes. Saddles were emptied. The captain shouted an order. The blue-clad cavalrymen dismounted and shought shelter.

All the long, hot day, crouched behind boulders, tree trunks or clumps of brush, the soldiers fought a bitter battle with the maddened braves who, despite their losses, still outnumbered them two to one. Charge after charge the soldiers withstood. Attack after attack was beaten off. But at heavy cost. When darkness fell, the captain, badly wounded, half his men dead, ordered a retreat. Slowly the troops withdrew down the canyon, taking their wounded with them. The Indians had fought them to a standstill, but just the same the soldiers had won. Cocha was dead, his power broken forever in Texas.

One trooper was left behind. Shot in the head, he had pitched into the heart of a dense clump of growth, senseless, overlooked by his comrades when they gathered up the other wounded.

His wound was really superficial, but when he recovered consciousness he wished it had proven fatal. For the surviving Apaches, as the last hoof clicked out of hearing down canyon, were creeping from cover and down the slopes. Two braves passed within a yard of where he lay concealed. Had they glanced down they could scarcely have missed seeing him. But they did not—their whole attention was centered on the canyon floor and the dead who lay there. Confident that the troops had departed, not to return, they built a huge fire.

The wounded trooper, shivering, scarcely daring to breathe, watched the braves passing methodically from body to body of the slain soldiers, taking scalps. The keen point of a knife would circle the top of the skull in a swift movement. A tug and the "scalp," a patch about the size of a silver dollar, would come free with a soft pop. The trooper grew sick at his stomach as he watched the gory work, but he made no move, knowing full well what would be his fate if he were detected.

Cocha's son, also named Cocha, tall as the great war chief himself, though only a boy in years, stood over his father's body, his handsome face, lighter in coloring even than his dead parent's, contorted with grief and hate, and swore an oath of vengeance. He strode to one of the dead soldiers and stripped the body naked. Standing the corpse against a tree trunk, he lashed it in an upright position. Drawing his knife, he criss-crossed chest and belly with swift cuts. Other cuts he scored from hip to ankle. The cuts were not deep, but had the victim been alive, he would have been screaming in agony.

Cocha plucked cartridges from his belt. With his strong teeth he wrenched the bullets from the shells and stuffed the powder into the body's mouth. He twisted a bit of dry sotol to form a fuse, lighted it and stepped back.

The powder exploded. The dead eyes popped out and hung on the dead cheeks. The lower half of the face was a shapeless pulp, with white shreds of shattered bone protruding through the flesh.

Beside himself with fear, the wounded trooper watched, unable to take his fascinated eyes from the awful ritual. It was, he knew, the rite of vengeance-torture, symbolizing what young Cocha would do to his father's killer when the time came. And the trooper also knew that did the braves discover him, *he* would undergo the torture, his quivering flesh knowing the anguish the passive corpse could not feel.

Suddenly young Cocha turned and walked straight toward his hiding place. From sheer terror the trooper fainted.

But young Cocha had not seen the wounded man lying but a few yards distant—he was merely looking for a suitable place for his father's grave.

The Apaches raised their fallen chief. With the moon hanging red over the cliffs and the canyon brimmed with lurid light, they buried him.

All night long the canyon walls echoed to the hoof beats of racing ponies, and when the quiet dawn stole over the mountains, no man could say where lay the grave of Cocha.

Full daylight had broken when the wounded trooper again recovered his senses. The canyon lay silent and deserted. Only the scalped and mutilated bodies and the hoof-beaten ground told that the Apaches had ever been there. Three days later, near death from exhaustion and loss of blood, he staggered up to the fort.

Captain Lije Bowman, recovering from his wounds, laughed heartily when told of the vengeance oath and the torture ritual. He wasn't afraid of young Cocha or any other Apache and maintained that the Indian bullet wasn't cast that could kill him.

Captain Bowman was right. Ten years later he died, comfortably in bed.

6

"And that was the end of Cocha and his tribe so far as Texas was concerned," Sime Bowman concluded his yarn. "Dad said that what was left of the bunch made their way west to Arizona before they stopped moving. Dad always admired old Cocha and he didn't hate him. He said Cocha fought for what he considered right and that was all there was to it. He respected Cocha with the respect one fighting man has for another. He said the Indians see things different from the way we see them and that it isn't right to hold their ways too much against them. Dad was a paid soldier with a job to do and he did it, but he didn't hate the fellers he fought."

"He had exactly the right notion," Slade said gravely. "We are all too prone to be intolerant of the other fellow when his customs, habits and ways of thinking are different from our own. Put ourselves in his place as far as we possibly can and we will regard him in a different light. Cocha had right on his side and we might as well admit it."

"My sentiments," Bowman agreed. He laughed a little. "During the past few months the darndest yarn has been building up in this section," he said. "There are folks who swear Cocha and his braves are riding again. Several old-times who claim to have seen him swear it was Cocha, nobody else. He was seen the night the Harlows lost a big herd from their southwest pasture, by a cowhand, an old feller, who happened to come along as they were shoving the herd toward Mexico. They didn't see *him*, or I reckon he wouldn't have lived to tell about it. It happened again the night before the gold wagons were robbed and the drivers and two guards killed. And the evening the stage was held up and a valuable express shipment lifted. The driver of the stage, who was shot and left for dead but got well, swore the leader of the bunch was Cocha dressed up in his war bonnet and everything. He was in the army in the old days and fought against Cocha, claimed to have known him well. Said he recognized him and it was Cocha and nobody else. He'd get so mad when folks argued with him, pointing out that Cocha had been dead for nigh to fifteen years, that he came near gunning a couple. He said how the devil could anybody be sure Cocha was killed in the big fight in Bone Canyon. He said Dad might have been mistaken when he figured he split Cocha's head wide open with his saber. Said he'd known men to get a saber cut that ripped half their scalp off but didn't kill them. And that the trooper who said he saw Cocha dead just made a mistake, that it was another chief who was killed. Darn nonsense, I'd say, but folks began to wonder, and they're still wondering. What do you think?"

"I'd say," Slade replied, "that some smart owlhoot is playing on Cocha's reputation. As you say, it doesn't make sense, but it works. Everybody along the Border knew perfectly well that Cartinas, the Mexican bandit leader, had been dead for many years; but a few years back a bunch began operating around Brownsville and Port Isabel. All of a sudden folks said Cartinas was riding again. He was 'positively identified' by half a dozen people who saw him. The Rangers finally rounded up the bunch, and there was no Cartinas among them, but just the same, to this day folks around there will tell you of Cartinas' raids less than five years back. Some outlaw with plenty of savvy is getting folks to believe that Cocha really is back on the job. The result, folks who should know better are looking for Cocha, concentrating on Cocha, and overlooking, the chances are, somebody right in their midst who is the real culprit. Yes, an old owlhoot trick, and it works."

"I've a notion you've got something there," Bowman conceded. "Me, I don't believe in no Cocha. I know darn well Dad killed him, more than fifteen years back."

"Wonder what became of Cocha's son?" Slade remarked irrelevantly.

"I think I can give you the lowdown on that," Bowman replied. "You know that over in Arizona they finally rounded up the Mangas and Mescalero Apaches and put them on a reservation. The older warriors decided to give up the fight and settle down and live peacefully on the reservation and take it easy the rest of their lives. But being shut up in a reservation didn't set over well with the young braves. They kept slipping away and raiding. Folks complained to the Indian Agent over there that there were Indians off the reservation. The agent always said no. Finally a salty old cowman wrote the agent telling him that if he'd visit the banks of Cripple Creek in the Animas Valley he'd find twenty Indians off the reservation. The agent investigated, and found twenty Indians off the reservation, and buried 'em. It was reported that young Cocha was among the twenty. Reckon it was so; he was the sort of young hellion who would slip away and raid. Anyhow, he was never seen around the reservation any more, nor any place else, so far as I've been able to gather. Yep, I guess he was one of the twenty the old cowman and his hands run down and did for."

As Slade was about to reply, a shadow fell across the table. Dirk Hudson, the saloon owner, placed two brimming glasses before Slade and Bowman.

"Something special, out of my own private bottle," he remarked pleasantly. "Here's luck to you and your friend, Sime."

Slade and Bowman lifted their glasses in acknowledgment. Hudson drank with them and it seemed to Slade there was a mirthful gleam in his usually inscrutable black eyes. Doubtless he had overheard their conversation and was amused by it. With a cordial smile that showed a flash of white teeth in his dark face, he walked back to the bar.

"Dirk sure is a fine feller," remarked Bowman, wiping his lips. "He never overlooks anything and is always doing the right thing at just the right time. That's how he built up his business, I reckon. Once a new feller drops in here he comes back."

"Good business, all right," Slade agreed.

"Dirk was smart, too, in talking Sol Bajo into helping out on the floor during busy times," Bowman added. "Sol knows cards and he's got a pair of eyes that doesn't miss anything. The dealers are careful when they know Sol has an eye on them; they don't pull any funny business. You know one crooked dealer can raise heck with the reputation of a place like this, even if he is finally caught up at his tricks. The same goes for bartenders, and Sol keeps a close watch on them, too—no pouring from the wrong bottle or slipping something over on a jigger who's had a snort too many."

Slade nodded agreement and asked a question. "I believe you said the stage was robbed of an express shipment a while back," he remarked. "What was the shipment?"

"Money," Bowman replied, "the Gonzales Mine payroll money, close to thirty thousand dollars. Funny thing about that—the Gonzales people were slipping it into town on the stage, figuring it would be safe that way. No guards, nothing to indicate there was anything in the coach worth stealing. But the hellions found out about it some way and grabbed it off. Quite a row about that one. The Gonzales people accused the express company of letting something slip, which the express company denied and hinted the leak was somewhere in the Gonzales office or at the Cooper bank. Sheriff Cross horned in and told them that if he'd been notified there was something of value on the stage, he'd have had deputies keeping an eye on it and it wouldn't have happened. The Gonzales crew countered that guards and deputies didn't help the Great Western gold wagons that were held up on the trail to Cooper, that guarding their gold just ended in three men being killed and another seriously wounded. Nice kettle of fish, everybody accusing everybody else of making mistakes, but the outlaws didn't make any—they got away with the dinero. Well, I reckon I might as well drag Arn away from that redeye and head back for the *casa*; got work to do tomorrow. Sure you won't ride with us?"

"Not tonight," Slade declined, "but I hope to get down your way later if I decide to stick around the section for a spell. Would like to see your goats."

"Cute little critters," Bowman answered. "It's a paying business, even better than cows, and this section provides prime goat range—plenty of good forage. We may end up with nothing but goats, although I was a cowman for a long time and you know that business gets a hold on you. Know anything about Angora goats?"

"Get mohair from them, and Morocco leather, don't you?" Slade replied.

"Uh-huh, and the wool is used with other fibers for linings, upholstery fabrics, velours and artificial furs. The wool doesn't shrink in milling. Gloves are made from the hides, too. Angora goats are mighty valuable. I got the notion of raising them over in the southeast, where I saw a big goat ranch and learned considerable about the business. Easier to handle than cows. If only some folks didn't have such dadblamed notions about 'em! One disadvantage, horses don't take to 'em; can't stand the smell and hate like the devil to get mixed up with 'em. Go plumb loco if they do; but they get used to 'em after a while. Our broncs don't pay 'em no mind any more. Well, I'm going to trail my rope; see you soon. My hand? Oh, I'd just about forgot about it. Back's a mite sore, but I reckon I'll pull through. Be sure and ride down to see us, and if you aim to coil your twine in the section, we could use another top cowhand. *Adios!*"

Slade watched his bulky form lumber through the swinging doors, the slender Arn trailing after him. Sime Bowman had done a lot of talking, but had told practically nothing about himself. Slade finished his drink and also left the saloon. Sol Bajo, standing at the end of the bar, waved his hand. Dirk Hudson was not in evidence at the moment. Slade headed for the stable where Shadow was quartered and let himself in with the key the stablekeeper had provided. He mounted the stairs to the little room over the stalls, humming under his breath. With his usual caution when in strange quarters, he stood to one side of the door as he swung it open. A bar of light from a bracket lamp on the wall revealed the room empty, his riding gear where he left it. He entered, struck a match and lit the lamp that stood on a table near the bed. He glanced at the bed and stiffened, staring at the thing which lay across the blankets.

It was a long, gaudily feathered, steel-tipped arrow!

Slade picked up the shaft and turned it over in his slim fingers. He studied it for a moment, then, with a mirthless laugh tossed it into a corner. It fell to the floor with a little clatter and lay there, the polished steel head winking evilly in the lamplight.

The window boasted a shade, the door a bolt. Slade drew one and shot the other. Fishing out the makin's, he sat down on the bed and rolled a cigarette with the finger of his left hand, contemplating the arrow the while.

The implication was plain enough. It was the old Indian message of enmity, a promise of death for the recipient. Whoever was raising the devil in the section was playing the Indian angle to a fare-you-well. The melodramatic act slightly amused and slightly irritated El Halcon. He wondered if whoever slipped the thing into his room expected it to scare him out of the section. He did not thiink so. Rather, it was likely a play to cause him to lean toward the local notion that Cocha or the ghost of Cocha was again leading his braves in raids on the hated whites.

As he smoked, he thought over the events of the past twelve hours. So far he considered he had learned practically nothing aside from the fact that two outfits were feuding. The Cocha yarn he dismissed as not worthy of consideration. Cocha was dead and he'd stay dead. Slade was not going to waste his time looking for resurrected Indian chiefs.

The most significant item, Slade thought, was Sime Bowman's story of the stage robbery, hinting as it did of somebody in a position to obtain information not put out for general consumption. Which in Slade's opinion tended to the belief that the outlaw bunch was operating out of Pearson, although Cooper, the railroad town, was not to be altogether discounted.

Well, it looked like he had his work cut out for him, but he had encountered similar problems before and was not inclined to consider that the present one posed insurmountable difficulties. Maybe he'd get a break. He went to sleep in an optimistic mood.

7

AFTER A LONG HARD DAY Slade slept late and awoke much refreshed. A quiet little restaurant across from the stable provided a leisurely breakfast, after which he strolled out to give the town a once-over.

Pearson was an up-and-coming pueblo, all right. Everywhere was bustling activity. Houses were going up, some of them quite substantial, and more streets were being laid out. Another stamp mill was in the course of construction. Slade saw something he hadn't seen for some time—several covered wagons that had rolled in since the evening before. It would appear the gold strike was a big one and, one that gave promise of enduring production. He got the rig on Shadow and rode up the canyon to where the mines were located, less than a mile from the site of the town, which had taken advantage of a widening of the gorge that provided ample room for expansion.

Already there were half a dozen producing mines, with preparations being made to explore still further lodes. Slade studied the workings with an engineer's eyes.

For Walt Slade was an engineer, and it was due to a series of unpredictable and untoward incidents that instead of working at his chosen profession he was wearing the silver star of the Rangers.

Walt Slade's father had been caught in the crash when, a few years before, the bubble burst, the trail herds stopped rolling north and cattle business in Texas temporarily went to the dogs. A year of blizzards and droughts completed the damage and the elder Slade lost his ranch. There was little doubt but that heart-breaking business reversals were responsible for his untimely death.

Young Walt managed to get through college, but the postgraduate course he anticipated taking to round out his education became impossible for the time being. Slade had worked

43

with Captain McNelty during summer vacations and when the commander of the Border Batallion suggested that he join the Rangers for a while and study in spare time, Slade felt it was a good notion. Long since he had acquired all he needed from private study, but Ranger work has a habit of getting under a man's skin. Once he is initiated into it he becomes loath to sever connections with the famous corps of law enforcement officers, and what had been intended to be a stop-gap job becomes a career.

So it was with Walt Slade. Eventually he'd be an engineer, but he was young and there was plenty of time. He'd stick with the Rangers for a while.

After inspecting the mines, Slade rode back down the canyon. Evening was drawing near, but he did not pause at Pearson. He was curious about that ledge from which the drygulcher had come so close to cashing in Sime Bowman. The thing had the appearance of being an ideal watch tower from which all that went on in the vicinity of the canyon could be observed. Slade wondered if the drygulcher had been stationed there for some purpose other than the killing of Bowman. He was inclined to believed it was the case and that the shot at Bowman had been but the taking advantage of an unexpected opportunity by someone desirous of doing away with the goat rancher.

The prairie was becoming gloomy when after leaving the canyon and circling north he reached the approach to the lofty bench; but he decided to go ahead and investigate while some light still remained.

The climb to the bench was steep but neither dangerous nor difficult. Upon reaching the crest, Slade found indications that the ledge had been traveled more than a little from time to time. A well-defined track ran through the tall growth and there were spots where an excellent view of the surrounding country was provided. He rode slowly and before he had doubled back to the east mouth of the canyon, full darkness had fallen. He knew, however, that soon there would be a full moon affording plenty of light for the return trip. He rode on till he reached the terminus of the bench at the canyon mouth. Here as the moonlight strengthened he could see north along the trail leading to the Harlow ranchhouse and south on the Cooper trail for some distance.

The place afforded a perfect lookout, similar to Castle Gap, where the Indians watched for approaching wagon trains or stagecoaches from the tall, windowed rock that gives the pass its name. Here a hidden watcher could signal to hidden confederates the approach of anything from the north or south long before it reached the canyon mouth. Which would enable them to attack from cover without leaving their places of concealment. Slade understood now how the gold wagons had fallen easy prey to the outlaws at just this spot.

As he sat gazing over the rangeland, he sensed movement on the Cooper trail. It resolved to a body of riders pacing their horses slowly from the south. Slade watched them approach and pass the canyon mouth, shadowy, unreal in the deceptive moonlight. It was too far to distinguish features, the faces being only whitish blobs. They appeared to wear the garb of cowhands, but he could not be sure. He counted seven in all.

That slow pacing interested Slade; the riders were little more than walking their horses, as if they were in no hurry to get where they were headed for and preferred not to get there before a specified time.

Of course they could just be a bunch of punchers heading home after a day in Cooper, but why that slow, purposeful gait? Cowboys didn't ride that way. As a rule they skalley-hooted whenever there was a chance to do so. The horses certainly did not appear exhausted, nor even tired. He watched them until they began to fade in the distance, his curiosity increasing by the second.

"Shadow," he told the horse, "if those gents keep on crawling like they are now, I believe we can make it back to the ground and maybe come within seeing distance of them if they have much of a ways to go. Maybe I'm being foolish, but somehow I got a hunch something isn't just as it should be. Come on, horse, let's go!"

Turning the black, he rode back along the bench as fast as was practicable. Reaching the lower ground, he sent Shadow diagonaling toward the north trail. He estimated it had taken little more than an hour to execute the maneuver. If the mysterious riders were proceeding as when they passed the canyon and had kept to the trail, he figured that in less than another hour he should bring them into view.

The night was brilliantly clear, the moonlight almost as bright as day; objects were visible for a great distance.

Mile after mile Slade rode at a fast pace, and did not sight the quarry. It began to look like they'd speeded up after passing the canyon. Shadow was toiling up a long slope, the crest of which was thickly grown with tall brush, when Slade became conscious of a sound, a crackling as of dry sticks burning briskly. It didn't take him long to recognize it as gunfire, a long ways off.

"Now what the blazes?" he muttered, and quickened Shadow's pace still more. As the trail wound up the slope the sound of shooting grew steadily louder. He reached the crest and abruptly reined in.

Below, the trail writhed down the opposite sag of the floor of a wide valley. A mile from the bottom of the slope Slade could see a big gray ranchhouse, very likely the Harlow *casa*. Over to one side a small building was burning fiercely. Across from the ranchhouse, which faced southeast, was a low ridge perhaps three hundred yards distant from the building. Along the crest of this ridge showed recurrent orange flashes. Answering flickers came from the ranchhouse windows. Somebody was staging a raid on the Harlow *casa*, if it was the Harlow *casa*, presumably the bunch he saw riding north past the canyon mouth.

The strategy employed was readily apparent to the Ranger. The small building had been set on fire to lure the occupants of the ranchhouse outside to extinguish the flames. Then they would have been mowed down by the raiders holed up behind the ridge.

. But evidently those inside the building had been a bit too smart to be caught in such a trap; they had seen through the scheme and hadn't come out. So the raiders were trying to smoke them out. Studying the solidly-constructed building, Slade was of the opinion they wouldn't have much luck.

Sitting his horse on the hilltop, he watched the battle. There was nothing he could do about it. To ride across the moonlit valley would be just a convenient way to commit suicide.

Intent though he was on the drama unfolding across the valley, El Halcon was still very much alive to his immediate surroundings. A slight rustling in the growth behind sent him whirling around in his saddle and swaying to one side.

Something struck his upper cartridge belt a smashing blow, ripped through his shirt and thudded on the trail a few yards distant. Slade jerked both guns and sprayed the growth with lead, whipping from the saddle to the ground in the flicker of motion.

Crouched in the shadow of his horse, thumbs hooked over the hammers of the cocked Colts, he peered and listened. No sound came from the brush, nor was there any sign of movement. He wondered if he'd done for the sidewinder. But perhaps he might just be waiting his chance. For minutes the Ranger remained absolutely motionless, every nerve strung to hairtrigger alertness, ready for instant action. And nothing happened. Then he heard, faint with distance, the click of rapid hoofbeats quickly fading to silence.

Slade straightened up with a disgusted growl. The hellion had made a getaway. Swiftly reloading his guns, he holstered them and strode to the object lying on the trail. He picked it up, a steel-tipped arrow that was a duplicate of the one left on his bed the night before.

"And if I hadn't turned around when I did, I'd have gotten it between the shoulders," he told Shadow. "As it was, it grained the skin over my ribs when it glanced off my belt and nearly knocked all the wind out of me. At close range this darn thing is worse than a gun. Makes no noise, and if the hellion chances to miss with the first one, he'll very likely drive a second one through you before you realize what's going on."

The explanation of the attack was fairly obvious. The raiders had left a man on the hilltop to warn them against possible interruption. The fellow, realizing he had but one man to deal with, had decided that murder was as good a method as any. Also it would have served to further the Cocha myth when his victim was found the next day, transfixed by an Apache arrow. Small wonder the superstitious folks of the section were believing that Cocha or his ghost was riding the hills again.

With an angry exclamation, Slade snapped the arrow in two with his powerful fingers and cast the piees aside. Abruptly he realized that something was missing. The stutter of distant gunfire was no longer quivering the air. He glanced toward the ridge facing the ranchhouse. It was dark and silent, with no more of the orange flashes splitting the gloom. The ranchhouse was also silent. The small out-building continued to burn merrily.

The sudden silence was ominous. Doubtless the raiders had heard the shooting on the hilltop and were wondering what it meant. Slade concluded he had better get out of there and without delay; there might be a shortcut from the ridge to the trail and he had no desire to tangle with half a dozen killers. The representative they had left to guard their backs had given evidence of cold-blooded disregard for human life. He could expect short shrift should he run into the bunch on the open trail. With a final glance around he mounted Shadow, turned him and rode back south at a fast pace, watchful and alert, his eyes probing the moon-silvered gloom, his ears straining to catch any unwonted sound.

As he rode, Slade pondered what he had seen and ex-perienced. On the face of it, what he witnessed fell into a familiar pattern. The Bowmans, in retaliation for the attack on young Arn the day before, had staged a raid on the Harlows. About what was to be expected, the enmity between the two factions being what it was.

But one obstinate thread refused to weave in properly. Had the attempt on his own life succeeded, it would have been out-and-out murder, no less. Which just didn't fit into the picture. The expected procedure on the part of the hidden watcher on the hilltop would have been to "wave him around" with a terse, "I'm lining up my sights on you, hombre. Turn tail and get back the way you come and don't stick your nose in other people's business."

Instead there had been a snake-blooded try at wiping him out. Began to look like whoever was raiding the Harlow ranchhouse, whether it was the Bowmans or somebody else, had something to conceal that wouldn't bear investigation.

Slade approached the lofty bench warily, but nothing happened and he rode on up the canyon to Pearson, reach-ing the mining town well past midnight. He stabled Shadow and repaired to the Ace High for something to eat. The place was quiet, with very few people around. Neither Dirk Hudson nor Sol Bajo was in evidence.

"Be like this for a couple more days," the head bartender explained. "Then look out! Three days from now is payday for all the mines and for the spreads in the section. The boys are saving up for the big payday bust. They'll bring the money up from Cooper, pay off in the afternoon and then Pearson will howl. Everybody taking it easy today. Sol is down at his horse ranch and Dirk rode off somewhere —he does a lot of riding. Used to be a cowhand and I reckon once a feller follows a cow's tail for a while he don't feel just right if he's away from a horse too long. Reckon you know how that is, eh?"

8

SLADE ate his belated dinner and then went to bed. Again he slept late and after breakfast returned to his room to smoke and think. He was curious as to whether Wes Harlow would ride to town and report the raid on his ranchhouse to the sheriff. Slade doubted if he would. The Bowman's or so he understood, did not report the attack on Arn Bowman. Appeared both factions preferred to settle their differences without recourse to the law. In fact, so far as Slade could gather, neither was in a position to complain. After attempting to kill young Arn on an open trail, the Harlows could hardly raise a row with the authorities over what had all the appearances of being retaliation for their own lawless act. Just the same Slade wanted to be around if either or both outfits came to town.

Later in the afternoon the Bowmans did come to town. Slade met them in the Ace High.

"Had a busy day yesterday and went to bed early last night," Sime told him. "Busy all this morning, too. Came in to order some supplies. Best to get all business transacted before payday when the only thing anybody will be interested in is raising the devil in one way or another. It's going to be a big one. I hear the mines are paying off a bonus this time, too. They promised it last month if production went over a set mark. Understand it did, way over, and the boys will be loaded with *dinero* which will be burning holes in their pockets. Not wanting to be set afire, they'll get rid of it as fast as possible," he added with a chuckle.

"You coming in for the bust?" Slade asked.

"Oh, sure," Sime answered. "Wouldn't miss it. That's why we tried to line everything up yesterday. We just about did but we were sure dog-tired when dark came. Could hardly keep my eyes open while I was eating my dinner.

Slept like a log and woke up feeling fine. What did you do yesterday?"

"Just a little riding and looking things over," Slade replied.

Bowman nodded his understanding. "Always liked to get the lowdown on a new section myself before deciding just where to coil my twine," he said. "Hope you'll figure to sign up with us. Maybe Wes Harlow'll hire you, though, just to keep us from getting you. Would be like him."

"I rather doubt it," Slade replied with a smile. "I think his opinion of me isn't overly high."

"Don't be too sure about that," Bowman answered. "Harlow is an old shorthorn, all right, but he knows the cow business and he's a pretty good judge of men, I'd say. And good hands are hard to come by right now, with big money to be made at the mines. Quite a few of the boys have turned in their ropes for a pick and shovel. Well, we're heading down to the general store and then back to the spread."

"You and Arn ride in alone?" Slade asked.

Bowman shook his head. "Nope, we got six of the boys with us," he answered grimly. "They're down the street a ways, sort of keeping an eye on things. Since what happened the other day, we're not riding alone any more. Be seeing you!"

Slade's eyes were very thoughtful as he watched the brothers pass through the swinging doors. It appeared that along with everything else plaguing the section, a first-class range war was brewing.

He recounted his conversation with Sime. If the elder Bowman had been putting on an act when he stated that he and his men had worked hard all the day before and had gone to bed early, it was a good one. Also it seemed he hadn't heard of Slade's run-in with Wes Harlow in the Alhambra saloon.

Slade dawdled over his drink a while and then also left the saloon. He sauntered along slowly in the direction of the big general store, in front of which a number of horses were tethered. He was almost opposite the building when the Bowmans and their hands came out. As they mounted their horses, Sheriff Jess Cross rode up and reined in. He had his sawed-off shotgun cradled in his arm and with him were three deputies who packed hardware.

"Now what?" Sime Bowman demanded.

"Nothing," returned the sheriff, "except we're riding to the forks with you fellers."

"We don't want you," Bowman stated flatly.

"Maybe not," retorted the sheriff, "but you're going to have us. I figure that very likely the Harlows will be riding this way and we're going along to prevent possible trouble. I don't think either you or the Harlows are big enough to buck the law," he added significantly.

"I don't aim to buck the law, now or any other time," Sime replied. "And we don't figure to start trouble with anybody, but if somebody else starts it we'll be there at the finish."

"Exactly," said the sheriff. "So I figure to go along before the start starts. You ready to ride?"

Slade chuckled as he watched the bunch ride out of town, Sime Bowman's back very stiff. Sheriff Cross was a salty proposition, all right, and Slade felt confident he would be able to take care of any trouble that came along, if he happened to be present when it developed.

However, in this particular instance the sheriff's fears proved groundless; the Harlows did not ride to town.

The following morning found Slade again riding down Bone Canyon. At its eastern mouth he turned south on the trail to Cooper, twenty miles distant.

As he rode, Slade carefully studied the trail and its environs. On the right it was flanked by the mountain wall, rugged, precipitous, practically unclimbable; but on the left it was paralleled by low ridges thickly covered with tall growth. Slade nodded with satisfaction from time to time as he studied the terrain. The trail was crooked for the most part, with many abrupt turns around projecting cliffs or juts of stone.

From time to time he passed empty wagons rumbling south, but as he drew near the railroad town he met loaded vehicles crawling north.

Upon reaching Cooper, Slade made his way to the local bank, which serviced the new town of Pearson as well as the surrounding country. He requested an interview with the president and after some hesitation, a clerk admitted him to an inner sanctum where sat the president, a pleasant middle-aged man with keen eyes. He was cordial and invited Slade to a chair.

"And what can I do for you, young man?" he asked.

"I wish to ask a question," Slade replied. "When does the stage carrying the Pearson mines' payroll money leave Cooper?"

The president jumped a little in his chair and looked a bit startled, involuntarily casting a glance at the closed door. Then he recovered himself and faced his interrogator.

"I am not at liberty to answer that question," he replied coldly. "Why do you ask?"

In answer, Slade slipped his Ranger badge from its pocket and laid it on the desk between them.

The president stared at the famous silver star on the silver circle. "Why—why—" he stuttered. "A Ranger! What does this mean?"

"A wire to Captain McNelty at Ranger Post headquarters will quickly secure confirmation, if you desire it," Slade replied.

The bank president shot him a shrewd glance, studied him for a moment, appeared to make up his mind.

"I don't think it is necessary," he said. "You've got the look and bearing of a Ranger, what a Ranger should be. The star is enough for me. But what does this mean? Why do you want to know about the payroll? Do you suspect an attempt on it might be made?"

"Frankly, sir, I don't know," Slade answered. "I have nothing definite upon which to base such a suspicion, but I understand it is an unusually heavy payroll, and strange things have been happening in this section of late."

"You're right on both counts," the president admitted. "It is a very large sum of money, and things have been happening; but in this particular instance I don't see how an attempt could hope to be successful. We are taking all possible precautions to safeguard the money. Nobody but trusted officials know just what stage will carry the money, and the coach will be heavily guarded. Two men outside and the driver, armed with shotguns and rifles, with orders to shoot to kill. Three on the inside of the locked coach, similarly armed. The stage leaving Cooper today will be guarded precisely as the one leaving tomorrow; but today's stage will carry nothing of value, while the payroll will be on tomorrow's coach."

Slade smiled a little. "Have you ever before dispatched the payroll money a day prior to the usual date?" he asked.

"Why, no, I don't believe we ever have," the official admitted.

"And isn't it reasonable to assume that an outfit as shrewd as the one operating in this section appears to be will take that into consideration and very likely see through your subterfuge "

The president drummed on his desk. "Now you've got me worried!" he exclaimed.

Slade proceeded to apply a clincher, "The Gonzales Mine money sent secretly by express didn't get through."

"There was a leak somewhere," the president declared. "Very likely at the mine."

"And it could happen again," he muttered, almost to himself.

"What do you advise?" he asked, raising his voice. "Shall we double the guard?"

Slade shook his head. "If six men can't fight it out with anything they might happen to run up against, twelve couldn't either. What you have to plan against is some smooth and unexpected strategem that will take the guards at a disadvantage and throw them off balance. What it could possibly be I have no idea, but I figure it's necessary to be on the lookout for anything."

"You are going to ride with the stage, then?" the president asked in a relieved voice.

Slade smilingly shook his head. "I doubt if that would help much," he said. "No, I won't ride with the coach, but I'll be riding."

The bank president looked puzzled, but he forbore asking questions, correctly deciding they would not be answered. Slade shook hands with him and departed.

"I'd appreciate it if you'd forget what I showed you today, sir," was his parting injunction.

"I will," the banker promised. Slade rode back to Pearson at a leisurely pace.

"If anybody happens to be keeping an eye on us, I've a notion this move will throw them off the track," he told Shadow.

Slade spent the following day loafing aimlessly about Pearson and its environs. He watched the heavily guarded Cooper stage roll in and with elaborate precautions deliver carefully wrapped packages to the various mines offices. That evening he appeared in the Alhambra, Ace High and other places. Old Wes Harlow was in the Alhambra, accompanied by Clem Atterbury, his grizzled range boss, and several of his Bradded H hands, all heavily armed. Slade nodded to Harlow and Harlow, not to be outdone in politeness, nodded back.

In the Ace High he had a drink with Dirk Hudson. The immaculately garbed owner was cordial and seemed in unusually good humor, his black eyes snapping, his lips wreathed in smiles. It seemed to Slade that he labored under a suppressed excitement. Which was not unnatural, Slade felt, with the hilarious pay night but a day off. Sol Bajo was his usual, quiet, dignified self. There was very little business.

"We're closing early," Hudson informed the Ranger. "Want to get a good rest tonight, for tomorrow we throw the keys away. She's going to be a lulu. No sleep tomorrow night."

It was long past midnight and to appearances, all Pearson was wrapped in sleep when Slade cautiously led Shadow from the stable, mounted him and, skirting the town, rode out of the canyon and south toward Cooper. He did not show up in the railroad town, however. Nor was he present when the stage pulled out shortly after full daylight.

But when the clumsy vehicle rolled northward along the rutted trail, El Halcon, mounted on his great black horse and taking advantage of every bit of concealment, rode the crests of the low ridges that paralleled the trail on the east.

The stage was drawn by six mettlesome horses and despite its weight and the condition of the trail, made fairly good time. Mile after mile flowed backward beneath its turning wheels, and mile after mile Slade paced the equipage, his eyes fixed on the vehicle with its two vigilant outside guards, one beside the driver, the second in the boot, and, he knew, three more inside the coach.

The miles from Cooper increased in number, and nothing happened. At each bend the guards held their rifles in readiness, eyes fixed on the turn, and on the straight-aways their gaze constantly roved the thickets and clumps of rock. The mouth of Bone Canyon was not many miles distant and still all was peaceful. Slade began to wonder if he was following a cold hunch; it was beginning to look that way. He relaxed somewhat, but still remained very much on the alert. Suddenly his eyes fixed on the trail to the north.

The stage was lumbering toward a bend where the trail curved around a great bulge of cliff. From where Slade rode both sides of the bulge were visible. Rolling swiftly out of the north and crowding the trail from edge to edge were a large number of little bobbing blotches. Behind them, urging them on, were seven mounted men; Slade watched their approach intently. At first he thought it was a flock of sheep, but as the herd drew nearer he realized his mistake. The bewhiskered, long-fleeced little animals were not sheep.

They were goats, a big herd of goats. Evidently the Bowmans were moving a shipping herd to Cooper. Slade relaxed again; then abruptly sat bolt upright in his saddle, leaned forward a little, peering with eyes narrowed against the sun glare.

"Shadow," he exclaimed, "those hellions shoving the critters along are wearing masks; sure as blazes they are! Now what the devil—"

Even as he stared in bewilderment, the "herders" suddenly surged forward, swinging quirts and ropes, slashing the little goats across their rumps. The alarmed creatures darted forward with frenzied speed, bleating hysterically, tearing toward the bend which the stage was just beginning to round. And abruptly Slade understood.

"Trail, Shadow, trail!" he shouted. He jerked the bridle sharply to the left and an instant later the big horse was tearing through the brush toward the distant trail, where the lumbering stage and the speeding goats were fast drawing together, with the bulge between them.

9

ON THE STAGE, the driver and the guards were in a cheerful mood. The more hazardous portions of the trail were behind them. Only a few miles distant was the mouth of Bone Canyon, Pearson and safety. They chatted together, called remarks to their three companions locked in the coach. Suddenly, however, the driver lifted his head.

"Something coming this way the other side of the bulge," he exclaimed. "Coming fast—sounds like horses! On your toes, boys!"

"What's that ba-a-in'?" asked one of the guards. "Sounds like sheep, but not like 'em, I wonder—holy blazes!"

The last ejaculation was shot from him as around the bend poured a multitude of frenzied little creatures giving tongue to irritation and protest.

Down upon the coach swooped the flying goats, too frantic with fear to turn aside. They butted into the legs of the horses, tumbled under their feet, bleating and squealing.

At the touch of the furry bodies and with the hated smell fuming in their nostrils, the horses went completely insane. They wheeled sideways from the trail, trying to escape the terror that plagued them. The front wheels of the coach cramped under the body as the horses plunged madly and tried to whirl back the way they had come, the top-heavy vehicle tipped up, reeled, went over on its side with a thunderous crash, flinging drivers and guards like stones from a sling to hit the ground with frightful force.

And around the bulge stormed masked men. They jerked guns and began shooting at the prostrate bodies and the overturned coach. With yells of triumph they swooped forward for the kill.

But their exultant whoops changed to howls of consternation as a great black horse raced from the brush flanking

57

the trail to come to a slithering halt. Topping the horse was
the tall form of El Halcon, a blazing gun in each hand.

Under that first flaming volley, three of the killers pitched
to the ground. The others fired wildly at the man forking
the weaving, dancing black horse. Slade's guns boomed again
and a fourth saddle was emptied. The three survivors
whirled their horses and fled madly back around the bulge.
Slade sent Shadow charging after them, and was immediately engulfed in the herd of milling goats.

Shadow didn't like goats any more than did the stage
horses, who were screaming with fright and plunging madly
to free themselves from the coach. Usually the most tractable
of beasts, Shadow took the bit in his teeth, whirled and dove
back into the brush. By the time Slade regained control of
him, skirted the bleating herd and swerved around the bulge,
the three fugitives were but distant brown smudges on the
trail, going like the wind and gaining speed at every jump.
Slade pulled Shadow to a halt.

"Hold it, feller," he told the snorting black. "If we head
after them they'll leave the trail and hole up somewhere;
they know the section and we don't. No sense in taking
foolish chances. Besides, we've got other things to look after.
Let's see how much damage is done back there. Don't worry,
I'll keep you away from those critters; they won't hurt you,
but you don't seem to know it."

He dismounted at the north edge of the bulge, left Shadow
where he was some distance from the goats, which had
quieted down and were beginning to browse the twigs and
leaves, and strode forward on foot.

There was plenty of damage done. The driver was thrashing about and groaning and swearing with a badly strained
leg. One outside guard lay white and silent beside him. The
other was on his feet, staring dazedly, blood streaming down
his face. The stage horses, one down, were a kicking, squealing tangle, but were pretty well exhausted from their struggles
and were becoming quieter. From inside the overturned
coach sounded groans, curses and angry yells.

"Hold it!" Slade shouted to the prisoners. "I'll get you out
as soon as I clean up this mess. Lend a hand," he told the
injured guard. "See if your pardner has a busted neck, and
try and quiet the driver; he isn't badly hurt."

The guard, shaking himself together, obeyed. Slade quickly

cut loose the struggling horses, got the fallen one to its feet and led them up the trail a little distance, where they'd be out of contact with the goats. His soothing voice and hand quieted them and although they still rolled their eyes, shivered and snorted, they remained where he placed them. He returned to the wrecked coach and tried the door, the lock of which was hopelessly jammed.

"Shoot the lock off," he told the imprisoned guards. "I can't take the chance of trying it from the outside; might plug one of you." He stepped back in the clear. "Let her go!" he called.

A muffled boom sounded inside the coach; the door jerked and rattled. A couple more shots and the lock flew to pieces.

'That should do it," Slade said. He gripped the handle and put forth all his great strength. "Get your shoulder against it," he called to the men inside. "All right, now, all together!"

A moment of struggle and the door flew open. Slade staggered, caught his balance, and held the door from swinging back. The bruised, bleeding and thoroughly battered inside guards crawled out spewing profanity and glaring around. Slade, who had knelt beside the stricken driver and guard, gestured toward the horses of the dead "herders." The well-trained animals had backed away from the goats but showed no indication of bolting.

"Catch those saddle broncs," he directed. "We'll rig up a stretcher between two of the stage horses and hustle these two men to town and a doctor. I'll strap up the driver's leg and he'll be okay, but I'm afraid the other fellow is in bad shape. Must have landed on his head and there are indications of fracture or concussion."

The old driver was filled with surly courage. After Slade had bandaged his injured leg tightly with strips torn from a shirt, he managed to get to his feet and hobble along with Slade to examine the bodies of the dead outlaws, ripping off the masks made from black handkerchiefs to get a look at their features.

Two were nondescript-looking individuals with little to differentiate them from other Border scum, but the other two were strikingly different. They were stocky, powerfully-built men with exceedingly dark complexions. They had lank black hair, broad faces, beady black eyes and thin-lipped, cruel looking mouths.

Slade raised his gaze to the driver's face, and in the old fellow's eyes was something very like fright.

"Feller, it looks like maybe Cocha really *is* riding the hills again," he muttered.

"That's rank nonsense and you know it," Slade answered. "Cocha's been dead fifteen years."

"Then maybe it's his ghost," mumbled the driver. Slade stared at him and shook his head. But even El Halcon felt a little queer as he dropped his eyes to the dead faces.

Without a doubt the two dead men were pure-blood Apaches!

The old driver glanced toward the browsing goats and back to the dead outlaws. He shivered a little.

"Feller, you sure got here just right," he said. "I'm getting scared all over. Those black devils wouldn't have left one of us alive, only before they'd got through with us we'd likely wished we'd been done in at the first shot. How come you got here at just the right time?"

"I was riding the ridge and saw what was going on," Slade explained. "I very nearly didn't get here in time. Didn't catch on at once, as I should have, for I saw a thing like this tried once before. That time with sheep; it didn't work, the horses bolted right through the flock. Angora goats are a lot better for a chore like this. Horses aren't afraid of sheep, but goats drive them frantic."

The driver glowered at the goats. "Part of those blasted Bowmans' holdings," he rumbled.

"But there is no proof that the Bowmans had anything to do with what was attempted," Slade quickly pointed out. "In fact, it doesn't seem logical that they would use their own beasts for such a purpose, knowing it would direct suspicion toward them if some corroborative evidence happened to be dug up."

"Guess that's right," admitted the driver, adding, "And it's pretty sure Sime Bowman wasn't with the bunch—none of them that big, so far as I could see. Nope, I reckon the Bowmans didn't have anything to do with it. Must have been old Cocha come back."

"Keep that in mind, about the Bowmans," Slade said, ignoring the final remark. "Keep that in mind and let's not have any loose talk when we get to town. That goes for you fellows, too," he told the guards who had joined them. Heads nodded sober agreement.

"We've got a stretcher rigged up that I figure will take care of poor Rolf," one said. "See if it isn't all right."

Slade decided that the makeshift stretcher would do. It was cradled between two stage horses and the strongbox containing the money was strapped behind the driver on the back of a third. The guards able to ride mounted the outlaw horses, which were docile beasts and of good stock. They bore meaningless Mexican burns and their rigs were ordinary.

Before the cavalcade got under way, Slade turned out the pockets of the dead men but discovered nothing of significance other than plenty of money. Their guns were ordinary and so were their clothes and riding gear.

With Slade leading the way, they headed for town. In the rear two of the guards had their heads together.

"I've heard it said that young feller is a owlhoot," one observed. "Well, if he is, I'm for owlhoots from now on."

"I'd say he's about as much an owlhoot as I am," the other snorted. "And anybody who says anything against him in my presence is going to get something to remember it by. Joe, we wouldn't be here right now if it wasn't for him."

Joe, who was the slightly-injured outside guard, nodded sober agreement.

"And did you ever see such shooting!" he marveled. "Those hellions were shot to pieces. I don't believe he scored a single miss. Well, I've heard folks say that El Halcon is the fastest and best shot in Texas. Reckon they knew what they were talking about. Wonder how he happened to come along so handy?"

"He didn't say, but I've heard he sort of makes a habit of being around at just the right time when trouble busts loose."

"And thank God for it!"

Pearson seethed over the attempted holdup. Some folks were inclined to link the Bowmans with the outrage because of the strategem of the goats, but it was agreed by most that the brothers should be exonerated. The description of two of the slain outlaws gave rise to further and grotesque speculations.

"They were Apaches, all right, no doubt as to that," declared one of the stage guards, an oldtimer who had fought Indians. "I tell you Cocha is riding again in this section, or maybe his ghost."

"Ghosts aren't downed by bullets," scoffers derided the suggestion.

"Maybe El Halcon used silver bullets," the guard contended stubbornly. "You can always down a ghost with a silver bullet. That is, if you can see him. Most often you can't, even though he's standing right behind you."

The statement was received with laughter, but just the same more than one oldster who had taken part in the wars with the tribes shot a surreptitious glance over his shoulder.

10

WHEN SLADE entered the Alhambra later in the afternoon, old Wes Harlow, his range boss and half a dozen of his hands were together at a table. Harlow glowered, then jerked a peremptory thumb toward a vacant chair.

"Sit down and have a drink," he rumbled as Slade strolled over to the table in response to the gesture.

"Don't mind if I do," Slade accepted, dropping into the chair. Harlow continued to glower at him over the rim of his glass. To Slade's amusement, his expression was a rather comical one of personal injury. He shook his gray head.

"Blast you, I can't make you out!" he complained querulously. "You got a near-owlhoot reputation that stretches all over Texas, but what you did today sure don't tie up with it."

"Perhaps I've reformed," Slade smiled.

"I ain't so sure, what with your taking up with the Bowmans and their blasted goats that destroy range," old Wes retorted.

"Harlow," Slade said, "you're talking like a confounded fool."

Old Wes glared and mouthed, but something in Slade's steady gray eyes so hard on his face averted what appeared to be an imminent explosion.

"You should know very well, or you would know if you'd taken the trouble to find out, that Angora goats don't destroy range," Slade continued. "They wouldn't even stray onto grassland; they won't touch grass unless they're starving. They don't graze, they browse. Leaves and twigs and berries are their provender. The Bowmans' hill pastures, covered with manzanita and the like, are ideal for Angora goats, while grassland is not."

"I've heard that before, but I didn't believe it," Harlow grunted.

63

"You're hearing it again, and you're believing it," Slade said.

The Bradded H hands were staring open-mouthed; never before had they heard their cantankerous boss spoken to in such a tone. Old Wes hammered the table with a ham-like fist.

"All right, the way you say it makes me have to believe it," he conceded, "but how about their fencing their holdings—barbed wire on what's always been open range!"

"And the time will come when you'll fence *your* holdings," Slade countered. "That is if you want to stay in business. The day of the open range is just about finished and progressive cattlemen all over Texas and elsewhere are realizing it. You'll go along with progress if you don't want to lose your holdings and have to go back to twirling a rope for a living, and you're a bit old for that."

Old Wes hammered the table some more. "You're the limit!" he bawled. "You're a pest! I wish I'd never laid eyes on you!"

He leaned forward abruptly and lowered his voice. "And here's something else maybe you'll argue," he said. "The other night those blasted Bowmans rode up and burned my blacksmith shop and gunned my ranchhouse."

"Have you any proof it was the Bowmans?" Slade asked quietly.

"Proof! What do I need with proof! If they didn't, who did?"

"I asked a question and I didn't get an answer," Slade replied. "Have you any proof the Bowmans did it?"

"No, I haven't," Harlow had to admit, "but—"

"And yet you immediately arrive at the conclusion that it was the Bowmans and nobody else," Slade interrupted. "It is neither the American way nor the Texas way to judge somebody guilty without proof just because we don't happen to agree with him. Your ancestors and mine fought a seven-year war against overwhelming odds to get away from that sort of thing, Harlow."

Old Wes gave a hollow groan and turned to his hands. "Please, boys, chase him off somewhere before I go loco as any bedbug that ever walked down a sheet," he pleaded.

The boys grinned, and showed no disposition to honor the request. Harlow turned back to Slade.

"See?" he wailed. "You even turn my own men against me! What the devil will you do next?"

"I'll tell you, boss," said lanky old Clem Atterbury, the range boss. "I've heard tell he's got just about the finest singin' voice in all Texas. He'll sing us a song, won't you, Slade? I'll fix it with the orchestra leader. You play the guitar, too, don't you? I'll get one. Okay?"

Slade nodded smiling acquiescence. Atterbury hurried to confer with the orchestra. He came back carrying a good instrument which he handed to Slade.

Old Wes Harlow lumbered to his feet, seized Slade by the arm and led him to the edge of the dance floor.

"Gents!" he bellowed, "we're going to have a little extra special entertainment. A song by a pest what had ought to be run out of the section. Maybe he'll sing so bad you will run him out."

All eyes instantly were turned on El Halcon, who was already the chief topic of conversation and conjecture all over town. The crowd hushed to listen.

Slade smiled at them, threw back his black head and sang a rollicking old song of the range that brought poignant memories to every man present, and as the great metallic baritone-bass soared and lilted under the high ceiling the hush intensified and the attention grew rapt and his hearers hung on every word.

The music ended in a crash of chords and a last ringing note and was followed by a roar of applause.

"Run him *out?*" howled a big cowhand at the bar. "We'll rope him and hogtie him if he tries to leave! Give us another, feller, give us another!"

Slade gave them another, and still another, ending the performance with a hauntingly sweet love song of Old Spain that caused more than one dance-floor girl to surreptitiously dab her lashes with a handkerchief and hardened old-timers to mutter something about the blasted smoke getting in their eyes. Slade handed the guitar back to the orchestra leader and returned to the table.

However, he did not sit down again. "Have to toddle along," he told Harlow. "Be seeing you again, I hope."

"Just a minute, Slade," Clem Atterbury said, "there's one little matter I'd like to clear up. I know you're feeling sort of contemptuous of four gents who'd try to down a single man on an open trail. I just want to say that we weren't trying to kill young Arn Bowman. We just aimed to throw a good scare into him. If we'd aimed to kill him, we would have. I know most cowhands are bum shots, but we have got a couple of jiggers who can dot a lizard's eye at thirty paces. And speaking of scares," he added with a wry chuckle, "the one you threw into us was a beaut. Took a minute to realize that you were holding high, too, and that you're the kind of a jigger who can lay a slug so close to a man without plugging him that he hears it say, real plain, 'you're next, brother, you're next!' Now I got that off my chest and I feel better."

Several of the Bradded H hands also looked like they felt better as they nodded solemn agreement to what Atterbury said.

Slade believed the range boss and his smile was all kindness.

"Hope we won't have occasion to scare one another any more," he said. "Be seeing you, gents."

"If you happen to ride north, drop in at my place for a surrounding," old Wes replied gruffly. "Maybe I won't pizen you, but I ain't promising."

As his tall form passed out through the swinging doors, Clem Atterbury, the range boss, turned to Harlow.

"Boss," he said, "do you know who he reminds me of—Rance!"

Wes Harlow's lined face abruptly looked old and wistful at mention of his dead son.

"Yes, he reminds me a lot of Rance," Atterbury repeated. "The same way of laughing at you with his eyes. The same way of saying things to you in a way you can't argue against. Taller than Rance was, but a lot like him, a lot like him."

"Yes," old Wes agreed heavily. "Yes, he is."

Outside the Alhambra, Slade paused to roll and light a cigarette. For some time he stood watching the workers from the mills and the mines stream into town. There were hundreds of them and all, with money in their pockets, seemed to anticipate a high old time.

Horsemen were riding into town, too, some with their mounts in a lather of sweat and their clothes thickly powdered with the dust of long and hard traveling. The spreads were sending their quota of hands to take part in the celebration; it appeared that everybody in the section was bent on a bust. Pearson was already beginning to growl and there was every evidence that the growl would quickly louden.

Slade visited the doctor's office, which was across the street from the Ace High, to inquire about the injured stage guard.

"A slight fracture and a bad concussion, but he'll pull through," the old doctor said. "Might have been different if you hadn't gotten him here in a hurry. As it was, I operated and removed the pressure on the brain before complications set in. You did a good chore, son. A couple of them, in fact. Maybe the larrupin' you gave those hellions will quiet them down for a spell."

"Maybe, but I doubt it," Slade replied.

"Never can tell, never can tell," said the doctor. "Sometimes a jolt like that will decide a bunch that a section is getting a mite too hot. By the way, how's Jim McNelty?"

"He's okay," Slade grinned. "You know him?"

"Yep, I know him," the doctor answered. "I also saw his lieutenant, once, and I don't forget faces."

"Sometimes it's good to forget what you don't forget," Slade chuckled.

"So I gather," the doctor agreed dryly, "and I'm mighty good at forgetting when I take a notion. But something for you to remember, sometimes there are folks who don't forget easily. Keep that in mind, son."

"I will," Slade promised soberly.

"Something else to remember," the old fellow added. "A doctor gets to know a lot about folks. You might want to drop around and have a little talk some time, if you happen to be a bit puzzled about somebody."

"There's somebody I'm puzzled about right now," Slade answered. "What is your opinion of the Bowmans, Doc?"

"Plumb honest and dependable, no matter what some folks say about them," the doctor instantly responded.

"I'm afraid you're right," Slade sighed. "Doc, you're not much help—yet."

Nevertheless, he was not displeased that the old frontier doctor had recognized him as a Ranger. Doctors did often get in touch with things not open to the average individual.

All in all, Slade was pretty well satisfied with the afternoon's work. He believed he had put a bug in old Wes Harlow's ear that would cause the cattle baron to do some serious thinking.

But with things in general he was far from satisfied. He had prevented a robbery, and, in all probability, some killings, but he still had not the slightest notion who had planned the outrage. He had been right in his surmise when he told the Cooper bank president that the outlaws would very likely see through the strategem of the double coaches or would obtain information relative to the subterfuge. They had done one or the other; no way to tell which. But they had substantiated his contention that there was an exceedingly shrewd individual handling the bunch, and somebody in a position to obtain supposedly secret information.

But who? Slade hadn't the slightest notion. With the Bowmans ruled out of the picture, as Slade was of the opinion they must be, who was left for him to suspect? Nobody, so far.

Crossing the street, Slade entered the Ace High, which was already well crowded. He saw Sime Bowman sitting at a corner table alone and joined him..

"I heard about it," said Bowman after he had ordered a drink. "No, not the robbery. That was a prime chore, too, but the other thing was more surprising. A feller who was up there came in and told me about it. He said you sort of hypnotized Wes Harlow, or something. How in blazes did you do it?"

"Appealed to his common sense and his sense of justice and fair play, with both of which I'm of the opinion he is well supplied," Slade answered.

"Maybe," Bowman conceded dubiously, "but he sure ain't shown much of either since I've been in the section."

"Perhaps he'll change," Slade said.

Bowman nodded his head, still dubious. "Maybe if you stick around long enough he will," he agreed.

"I'm very much of the opinion he will," Slade nodded. He let the full force of his level gray eyes rest on the rancher's face.

"Sime," he said, "I want to ask you something, and I want a straight answer—did you go up and gun Harlow's ranchhouse the other night?"

Sime Bowman's mouth opened, his eyes bulged. His astonishment was so ludicrous that when he spoke, Slade did not in the least doubt he was telling the truth.

"Heck, no!" he sputtered. "Why should I do such a thing? It would be plumb loco, and I ain't the kind that sneaks around in the dark throwing lead at folks and maybe plugging the wrong one. Why'd you ask me such a question?"

"Because somebody did gun the Harlow ranchhouse the other night and burned their blacksmith shop," Slade replied quietly.

Bowman continued to stare at him in bewilderment. "How you know?" he asked.

"I was up that way and saw it done," Slade answered.

Bowman shook his head and swore. "Who *would* do such a thing?" he demanded.

"I don't know," Slade admitted, "and I certainly wish I did know."

"But why would they do it, whoever they are?" Bowman persisted.

Slade again fixed Bowman with his gaze. "In my opinion, the notion is to stir up trouble between you and the Harlows," he said. "Why? That's another question I can't answer, but it looks like somebody would be very pleased if you killed Wes Harlow or Wes Harlow killed you. And don't forget that somebody took a shot at you from that bench east of the canyon and came close to making a finish job of it. It would appear you have incurred the enmity of someone who has no compunctions about committing murder."

"Well, I'm darned if I know who," Bowman sputtered. "I've had no real trouble with anybody other than the Harlows. Even the old-timers who side with them have kept out of the row and say they want no part of it. The same goes for the fellers who lean toward us. I can't understand it."

"I can't either," Slade admitted, "but it appears to be an indisputable fact. So forget all about your row with the Harlows and concentrate on keeping your skin free of air holes. I suppose you have some of your men here with you tonight?"

"That's right," Bowman nodded. "Several of the boys are over at the bar right now."

"Have them with you whenever you ride, especially at night," Slade advised.

Bowman rasped his chin with his forefinger, scratched his bristling head.

"Confound it, you've got me scared!" he admitted frankly.

"Stay scared, and stay alive."

"I'll promise to do the first and try to do the second," Bowman answered. "And I've a notion," he added, "that you made some bad enemies yourself today."

"Perhaps," Slade agreed composedly.

Bowman gazed at him and shook his head. "Don't believe you've got a nerve in your body," he declared.

11

As the loving blue dusk began to sift down from the hills, the growl of Pearson welled to a rumble. The redeye men had been drinking all afternoon was beginning to get in its licks. Sime Bowman glanced around the crowded Ace High.

"Going to be a big night, all right," he observed. "The boys are already feeling their oats. Sheriff Cross rode up from Cooper and brought three of his deputies along; and he swore in a lot of specials. I understand he sent a wagon down the canyon to bring in those bodies; wants to put them on exhibition in case somebody might recognize them. Seemed plumb flabbergasted when he heard what happened. Reckon he wants to have a talk with you. 'Peared mighty puzzled about you; hardly knew what to say."

Slade smiled but did not otherwise comment.

"What about your goats they used to stampede the stage horses?" he asked suddenly.

"Oh, the boys rounded 'em up and shoved 'em back to pasture," Bowman replied. "They're easy to handle. The hellions must have widelooped 'em during the night and hid them in the brush somewhere till they were ready to use them. Funny, ain't it, their broncs didn't seem to mind the little devils much. Looks like they must have sort of conditioned their horses to goats."

"It does look sort of that way," Slade agreed thoughtfully.

"Suppose we have something to eat while there's still a chance to get it," he suggested. "At the rate business is building up it won't be long till eating is out of the question."

"A prime notion," agreed Bowman. "I'm beginning to feel like a few snorts myself and it's best to lay a foundation of chuck before going in for serious drinking."

They ate together, smoked a couple of cigarettes. Then Slade left the saloon for a while and sauntered out to give the town a once-over. He had a premonition that there would be lively doings before daylight and perhaps some skullduggery buildup. There would be some fine opportunities for somebody with the wit to take advantage of them; and whoever was operating in the section certainly didn't lack for wit. He walked to the edge of the town, where it was quiet, and for some time stood leaning against a hitchrack, thinking.

Why did somebody want to kill Sime Bowman? Why did somebody want to foment trouble between Harlow's Bradded H and Bowman's Lazy B? So far as he had been able to learn there was no apparent reason. The Harlow-Bowman feud was one common enough to cattleland, the sort of thing that is fought out open and above-board, with each side insisting itself right and the other fellow wrong. Such rows could be bloody enough, but seldom were they accompanied by sneak killings or undercover tactics of any kind. When men believe they are right in what they are doing, they usually don't take the trouble to try to cover up. More likely, in fact, to brag about their acts and let everybody, especially their enemies, know about them. The raid on the Harlow ranchhouse had been secretive, under cover of darkness. The attempt on Sime Bowman's life had been from ambush, and Slade understood that the shot which came close to killing Tom Harlow, old Wes' younger brother, had also been fired by a hidden drygulcher. Slade just couldn't see either the Bowmans or the Harlows indulging in such practices.

Of course a man's workers sometimes got out of hand and did things the boss wouldn't condone, but Slade did not believe that applied in this case. The respective outfits appeared to take but a mild interest in the row, ready to string along with the boss but not enough aroused to take the initiative. But without a doubt somebody was out to get Sime Bowman, and very likely his brother, also, and ready to employ any method that came to hand. But why? Unless there was a chapter in Bowman's life he didn't see fit to reveal, and Slade didn't believe there was, there appeared no obvious explanation of the business, no explanation of any kind, for that matter. And yet, Slade was confident that in some manner the affair tied up with the lawless acts being committed in the section. He regretted that the out-

laws he downed in the course of the abortive stage robbery
didn't live long enough to do a little talking. Might have
served to clarify matters—that sort would usually blab to
save their own necks. To the undoubted fact that he himself was in deadly danger, he gave little thought. Perhaps
if the bunch got mad enough at him they'd lose caution
and do something to tip their hand. Consoled by the dubious prospect, he made his way back to the busy sector of
the town.

It was busy, all right. Pearson's growling rumble had
grown to a bellow and already there was action a-plenty.
The clean tang of fresh sawdust on the floors was befouled
with the reek of spilled whiskey and in more than one place
by the raw and piercing smell of spilled blood. There had
been fights during the afternoon, none of a serious nature.
A couple of cuttings. A shooting in the Blue Wolf that
was squelched before it really got under way, and a number of wrangles that were productive of black eyes and
busted noses, and which were forgotten almost as soon as
the floor men in the bars had hurled the combatants apart.

But now, as the night descended, nerves were getting
raw, tempers roughened, judgment befuddled. Men began
walking stiff-backed and truculent of eye, their hands close
to the weapons swinging at their belts. Bartenders and floor
men became more alert. The special deputies were on the
lookout for trouble.

It was not long in coming. In the Last Chance, guns
suddenly flamed. When the smoke had cleared away, three
men lay in the sawdust, badly wounded. Sheriff Cross arrested
the uninjured participants in the affair and locked them in
the calaboose. Others followed and soon the little one-room
jail was crowded to suffocation. Three rowdy young cowhands who liked to smash glassware refused to obey the
sheriff's order to behave and were collared by the deputies
and hauled off. There was no room for them in the jail,
so the sheriff secured leg irons, of which he had brought
along a plentiful supply, and tethered them to stout posts
driven in the ground in front of the jail. A little while later
there was a prodigious bumping and clattering on the board
sidewalk outside the Ace High. The three cowboys filed in
and demanded whiskey, which a grinning bartender served
them. Unable to free themselves from the leg irons, they

had managed to work their posts out of the ground and drag them along with them.

Walt Slade, who happened to be in the Ace High at the moment, laughed till the tears hopped down his bronzed cheeks. The touch of comedy was welcome and such she-nanigans were no affair of his. It was up to the sheriff and his aides to quell the local disturbances; Slade had more serious things to contend with.

Trouble started in the Ace High. A half-breed miner leaned across a poker table, steel flashing in his hand. Before he could rip out the throat of the man opposite him, an ice-eyed dealer flipped a short-barreled derringer from his sleeve and smashed the hand that held the knife. The half-breed dropped his steel with a howl of pain. His adversary, who had "reached" instantly, slid his six-gun back into its holster as he stared into the black muzzle of the dealer's sleeve gun. The dealer flipped the wicked little weapon back into his sleeve and shuffled the deck as calmly as if nothing had happened. The glowering half-breed peered at his hole card, clumsily fingering his chips with his left hand. The man he had tried to knife bet two blues and, a moment later, gathered in the pot. The half-breed won the next one, and the pair grinned across the table at each other, their differences forgotten in the excitement of a good hand of cards.

"You'll notice Sol Bajo was right behind that dealer when the trouble started," Sime Bowman observed to Slade. "He's right on his toes every minute. But I've a notion he doesn't care much for this sort of thing."

Slade thought so, too. Bajo's deeply blue eyes were somber, his lips unsmiling.

"That name of his!" Slade commented. "It's an unusual name, but I'll swear I've heard it somewhere before, although in what connection I can't recall."

"Does sound sort of funny," Bowman agreed. "The last part has a Spanish sound, but the first part sure don't.

"Dirk Hudson's acting all het up about something, too," he added. "He's frownin' like a thunder cloud."

Slade had already noticed that the saloon owner looked to be in a bad temper. His dark countenance wore a scowl and he appeared nervous and ill-at-ease. A moment later he paused at their table with a word of greeting.

"What's the matter, Dirk?" Bowman asked. "You look grumpy."

"Oh, I've had a raging toothache all day," Hudson replied. "It's giving me the devil and nothing seems to do it any good."

Bowman clucked sympathetically. "Sure ain't nothing to sneeze at," he agreed. "I've had 'em, and they're no fun. But look at all the money you're making tonight. That had ought to help."

"I've a notion a millionaire with the bellyache is just as unhappy as the rest of us would be," Hudson replied with a wry smile as he walked away.

Walt Slade moved from place to place, quiet, watchful, his keen gaze studying faces and actions, searching for anything significant or out of the ordinary. He had a hunch that something was going to happen before the night was over, something other than the usual rows and general fooforaw to be expected on a payday in such a town.

He was constantly forced to turn down offers of drinks that were showered upon him wherever he showed up.

"You see, it's like this, feller," a big miner explained. "Us fellers figure if it wasn't for you we wouldn't be having our bust tonight. Those scalawags would have gotten away with our money and we'd have had to put off our celebration till they got some more sent up from Cooper. We want to show our appreciation."

Slade took a sip from a glass to satisfy him, before he moved on.

It was past midnight when he entered the Alhambra. There he found the biggest crowd yet, but rather more orderly than the average. The ranch owners, mine officials and business people of the community did their drinking in the Alhambra, the miners and cowhands mostly preferring the more boisterous places farther along the street.

Wes Harlow and his men were still at the big table in the back of the room and appeared little the worse for wear but enjoying themselves in their own way. Harlow gruffly invited him to draw up a chair, which Slade did.

Old Wes looked at him expectantly. "Well, I suppose you've been hobnobbin' with Bowman," he remarked.

"Yes, I saw him a little while ago," Slade said. "Incidentally, he said he did not gun your ranchhouse the other night."

Old Wes swore querulously. "Then I reckon he didn't," he conceded. "No matter what else that scut is, I don't figure him to be a liar. What in blazes *is* going on in this section, anyhow?"

"I wish I knew," Slade replied. "Mr. Harlow, can you call to mind any bad enemy who might desire to do you an injury?"

Old Wes shook his head. "Hanged if I can," he replied. "Back in the old days, me and some of the boys had ruckuses, but that was all over long ago. We're all getting too old for such foolishness and we talk 'em over sometimes and laugh about 'em. No, I can't think of a soul who would deliberately set out to make trouble for me. I know I don't see eye-to-eye with some of the new folks who have been moving in, but aside from the Bowmans I ain't had a row with any of 'em. It's beyond me."

"Beyond me, also," Slade said. "It just looks like somebody is very anxious to stir up trouble between you and the Bowmans, as I told Sime a little while ago. I'd say somebody would be very pleased if you and Sime gunned each other to a finish."

Harlow swore in weary disgust. "Sometime I wish I'd died a-bornin'," he declared. "I'd hoped to live out my last days in peace and comfort, but I sure ain't doing it."

Slade smiled slightly and thought of a Biblical quotation that fitted the case precisely, "As ye sow, so shall ye reap," but refrained from putting it in words.

"Drinks!" Harlow bawled to a passing waiter. "I'm just in the mood to get ossified like everybody else with a mite of sense is doing. Down 'em, boys! I'll crave company when I'm sufferin' tomorrow!"

The drinks were forthcoming. Slade sipped his and his glance continually roved over the crowded room.

"Here comes Bob Higgins, the owner, with another satchelful," observed Harlow. "He's been packing money into the back room all night. Reckon that old safe of his is plumb stuffed. Lots of miners always leave part of. their pay with Bob, so they won't be clean busted come tomorrow."

The corpulent and cheerful Alhambra owner waddled

past the table, carrying a small black valise. He threw Harlow and the others a cordial word and passed into the back room which was close to the table, leaving the door open a crack. Slade absently watched his broad back disappear from view. Abruptly he leaned forward, his eyes narrowing.

Above the racket in the saloon, his keen ears had caught what sounded like a gasping cry followed by a soft thud as of a man's body striking the floor. He was sure the noise came from the back room. He shot from his chair and reached the door in two long strides. He widened the opening, slipped through and closed the door behind him.

The room was furnished with a table, a number of chairs and a big iron safe upon which stood a lamp; the door of the safe was open. On the floor lay Higgins, a man wearing a black mask in the act of straightening up beside him. Another masked man was widening the safe door.

12

SLADE went for his guns, but the man by the safe acted with the speed of light. His arm swept the lamp to the floor; darkness blanketed the room. A shot blazed as Slade hurled himself sideways and the bullet ripped the skin of his neck. He fired at the flash, ducked low and fired again as an answering report thudded a slug into the wall above his head. There was a patter of feet, the bang of a door hurled open and terrific crashing of breaking glass. Slade sent two bullets at the sound, shifted position and stood with his thumbs hooked over the hammers of his cocked guns, listening intently. Again he thought he heard the sound of running feet, outside this time.

The inner door banged open and Wes Harlow loomed silhouetted against the light, beside him Clem Atterbury, the Bradded H hands crowding behind them.

"What the devil's going on here?" Harlow bellowed.

"Come in and shut the door, and have your men keep the crowd out," Slade directed. "Strike a match, Atterbury."

Old Wes banged the door shut and fumbled the bolt. The Bradded H hands were left on the other side. A match flickered and by its faint light Slade saw that the back door of the room stood wide open. The window was smashed to splinters. He glided to the door, guns ready for instant action, and peered into a dark alley. There was nobody in sight.

Atterbury struck another match. Slade spotted the lamp on the floor, its chimney shattered but the bowl intact. He righted it, struck a match himself and touched it to the wick. A smoky flare cast a lurid glow over the disordered room.

"My God! Is poor Bob done for?" exclaimed Harlow.

Slade knelt beside the stricken owner, who was bleeding profusely from a gashed scalp but was already thrashing

78

about with returning consciousness. He swiftly examined the wound, wiped the blood from Higgins' face with a handkerchief.

"Anybody got another clean one?" he asked.

Atterbury produced a second handkerchief and with it Slade padded the wound in an effort to retard the bleeding.

"I don't think he's badly hurt, but send for the doctor," he said.

Old Wes opened the door, bellowed an order and closed it again. Higgins opened his eyes and gazed dazedly about.

"Take it easy," Slade cautioned. "I think you're okay, but we're not taking any chances."

With Slade's assistance, Higgins struggled to a sitting position. He sat for a moment with his bloody face in his hands. Then, his strength recovered somewhat, he raised his head.

"What happened?" Slade asked.

"I'm hanged if I know," Higgins mumbled his reply. "I was just shutting the door when something hit me. That's the last I remember."

"Evidently the hellions heard you coming and ranged alongside the door and let you have it soon as you stepped in," Slade interpreted the attack.

"Did they get the money?" Harlow asked.

Slade arose and passed to the safe. "Don't think so," he announced. "The inner door isn't even open. And here's Higgins' satchel on the floor, and it hasn't been opened. He came in just in time to interrupt them before they got really started."

He gazed at the safe, turned to the saloonkeeper.

"Did you leave the safe unlocked when you were in here last?" he asked.

"I don't think so," Higgins replied. "Can't be plumb sure, but I make a habit of locking it when I leave the room."

Slade nodded. "It hasn't been forced," he announced. "If it was locked, they must have worked the combination, something rather unusual for this part of the country. Who besides yourself knows the combination?"

"My head bartender knows it," Higgins replied, adding instantly, "but I'd trust Bert with my life."

Slade nodded. "And was there ever anybody in this room when you worked the combination?"

"Why, yes," Higgins said. "We have a meeting of the boys here every now and then, and sometimes I open the safe to get something out."

"What boys?" Slade asked.

"The other saloon owners," Higgins explained. "Dirk Hudson, Bajo, his floor man; Wolver and his head bartender; Wilkins, Carrington, Mason, and others."

"I see," Slade said. "So any one of a dozen men who happened to have sharp eyes and a good memory could ascertain your combination."

"I reckon that's so," Higgins admitted, "but feller, surely you ain't acusing the boys of doing such a thing."

"I'm accusing nobody," Slade answered. "However, the fact remains that somebody tried to rob you and took a chance of killing you when you interrupted them. And to all appearances, somebody worked the combination of your safe. See how the situation stands?"

Higgins nodded and nursed his aching head. Old Wes wagged his own grizzled top piece and stared at Slade.

" 'Pears you sort of make a business of saving people's cash, son," he remarked. "Twice in twenty-four hours. I aim to have Jess Cross make you a deputy. You've done more in one day than him and his whole kit and kaboodle have done in a year."

"I just happened to be around when something was happening," Slade smiled.

"Uh-huh, just happened around at just the right time," Harlow agreed dryly. "Reckon you just *happened* to take a notion to barge into this room when you did."

"I heard something," Slade admitted.

"Yes, and the rest of us didn't hear it, and, the chances are wouldn't have done the right thing quick enough if we had heard," grunted Harlow. "Uh-huh, you ought to be a peace officer instead of sashayin' around over the country taking the chance of getting into trouble."

The door opened and the doctor hurried in. He examined Higgins' wound and proceeded to cleanse and bandage it.

"Nothing serious," was his verdict. "You'll have a head-ache, but not as bad a one as those hellions in the outer room. How'd it happen?"

He was told and indulged in some vivid profanity. "What a night!" he concluded. "I've been on the jump ever since the middle of the afternoon. Just finished plastering up Dirk Hudson and picking broken glass out of his face."

"Broken glass?" Slade repeated.

"Uh-huh," said the doctor. "Come in breathing like he'd run a while, with blood streaming down his face. Said he'd stepped outside for a breath of air and some loco hombre threw a bottle across the street. It hit the wall right alongside his head and peppered him wtih splinters. Had one pretty bad gash, and some bits stuck in his skin. Said he chased the hellion half across town but lost him in the dark."

Slade nodded. Involuntarily he glanced across the room at the shattered window. However, he did not comment.

"Well, guess we might as well go back to our drinks," suggested old Wes. "Everybody'll want to know what happened; what'll we tell 'em?"

"The truth," Slade said. "There's nothing to cover up and nothing to be gained by doing so. And the sheriff should be notified of what happened. This is a bit more serious than payday brawls."

"I'll send one of the boys to hunt him up," Harlow offered. "And you'd better have that window patched and set somebody in here with a gun for the rest of the night, Bob. Don't reckon the hellions will pay you a return visit, but anything is liable to happen on a night like this. Let's go!"

In the outer room they were bombarded with questions which they answered without reservation. Admiring glances were cast at Slade, howls of indignation went up and for a brief period the frustrated robbery was animatedly discussed.

But not for long. The drinks were potent, the eyes of the dance-floor girls bright, the spots on the cards brighter still. Soon the outrage was forgotten.

The Bradded H hand reappeared, with Sheriff Cross in tow. The sheriff gave Slade a puzzled look, accepted a chair and a drink.

"Now tell me about what happened," he requested.

Slade told him, tersely but in precise detail.

"You didn't get a good look at them?" Cross asked.

"Not more than a glance," Slade replied. "They were masked and about all I can say is that the one beside Higgins was squat and broad, the one by the safe tall. I think they wore dark clothes."

"Cowhand clothes?"

"No, store clothes," Slade answered. "I was sort of busy and didn't have time to count the buttons."

Clem Atterbury chuckled; the sheriff flushed a little.

"So you wouldn't be able to recognize them if you saw them again," he observed. Slade shook his head. He asked a question of his own.

"Did you bring those bodies in from the canyon? Yes? Has anybody recognized them?"

"A couple of bartenders who had time to run over to the office think they may have served the white ones at some time or other," the sheriff replied. "They ain't sure, though, and nobody rec'lects seeing either of the breeds."

"They're not breeds, but pure-blood Apache Indians," Slade said quietly.

"That's what old Tol Brady, the stage driver said," admitted the sheriff. "He ought to know—he fought old Cocha when he was alive."

"Maybe he's still alive," a Bradded H hand muttered.

"That's darn foolishness, and you know it," snapped the sheriff.

"Maybe," conceded the cowboy, a grizzled oldster.

"No maybe about it," the sheriff declared emphatically. "Everybody who has any sense knows Cocha is dead."

"Ain't nobody ever found where he was buried," the cowboy insisted stubbornly. The sheriff gave him a disgusted look.

"And what does that prove?" he demanded.

"Nothing, 'cept that nobody knows for sure Cocha was killed in Bone Canyon," said the cowboy. "John Rader, who drove the stage when the Gonzales payroll was lifted, swears he saw Cocha heading the robbers, and he knew Cocha when he was raiding."

"Rader was shot to pieces and delirious when he was picked up," countered the sheriff. "He didn't know what he was saying."

"Uh-huh, but he kept mumblin', 'It was Cocha! Cocha himself come back from Hades!' "

The sheriff threw out his hands. "I guess when folks get

an idea fixed in their heads there's no rooting it out, no matter how loco it is," he said.

"Well, be that as it may, there's no doubt but that a mighty bad and a mighty smart bunch is operating in this section," put in Wes Harlow. "You ought to do something about it, Jess."

"I'm doing all I can," answered the sheriff. "And I wrote Jim McNelty for Rangers to help me."

"So did other folks, only we ain't seen none so far," said Harlow. He jerked his thumb toward Slade and added, "If this young feller will just stick around a while, maybe we won't need 'em."

The sheriff did not look particularly convinced, but he refrained from arguing the point.

"You did a couple of good chores today, son," he commended Slade, "but be careful how you take the law in your own hands. It's liable to get you into trouble some time." Old Wes Harlow snorted derisively.

The sheriff wiped his mustache and stood up. "Have to move along," he said. "Things are getting worse by the minute. I'm trying to keep 'em under control, but it's pretty nigh a hopeless task. There'll be some killings before morning or I miss my guess. Be seeing you."

"Jess is a good man," Wes Harlow observed. "He'll do the best he can, but it would take a regiment to keep those rock-busters in hand. They sure do raise the devil and they're salty hombres. I wonder if it will always be like this?"

"I doubt it," Slade replied. "It's always this way while a strike is comparatively new. A big strike of any kind brings in turbulent characters, but after a while they settle down or drift off and things regain a normal balance. It was that way at Tombstone and Bisbee and other places. And at Abilene and Ellsworth and Dodge City when the great trail herds were rolling north. Part of the price we pay for progress."

"Hope you're right," said Harlow. "I'll have to admit I still sort of like shindigs of this sort, but sometimes I pine a bit for the nice quiet sessions we had at Cooper before they built this darn town."

Slade chuckled under his breath. He felt that old Wes' "pining" wasn't very deep-seated. There was nothing to prevent him doing his celebrating in Cooper instead of Pearson. The old jigger still had warm blood in his veins.

"Getting back to what we were talking about a while ago," observed Harlow, "I just can't figure who the devil would want to get me into a bad row with the Bowmans and probably get me killed."

"Is there anybody who would profit by your death?" Slade asked.

"Only my girl—my daughter—and I can't see her getting the old man cashed in for a few acres," Harlow replied.

"Would be a bit unorthodox, to say the least," Slade smiled "I wonder how about the Bowmans."

"I've heard that the only close living relative they have is their old mother," put in Atterbury. "Sort of doubtful if she'd go for drygulching."

Slade shook his head. The matter grew more enigmatic all the time. "Well, I think I'll move along and look things over a bit," he said.

"Ride up to my place when you get time," Wes Harlow invited. "I got a prime cook."

"That's an inducement," Slade admitted. "I'll very likely take you up on it soon."

As the night wore on, the roar of Pearson assumed a shriller note. It had been a deep-toned animal growl of lusty life unleashed. Now it was the piercing howl of nerves strained to the breaking point, of hysteria approaching the cold blackness of utter madness. The streets were full of reeling, staggering men. The dance floors were scenes of wild abandon. The orchestras blared raucous discords, and nobody noticed. At the gaming tables men fingered stacks of gold pieces with trembling hands, cursed as they shoved them toward the cold-eyed, iron-nerved card sharps, peered wildeyed at the cards dealt them, and cursed again.

The bars were jammed with a mass of sodden, drunken humanity. The crash of a pistol shot and the scream of a wounded man were hardly heeded. The bartenders had ceased to measure drinks or draw corks. They snapped the necks of the bottles and gushed the fiery liquor over the splintered glass, careless of bleeding fingers. They forgot to make change, and no one cared. They forgot to take pay for the drinks they poured, and no one cared.

The spirit of utter abandon that pervaded the roaring workers infected others. The dealers grew careless, began taking the same chances as the reckless players. They forgot to win or lose with icy indifference and mingled their curses with the others. Women who had greedily clutched at gold during the early hours now cast it away with as little thought as had the men from whom they took it. Nothing was worth the effort to save.

The drunkenness was more than the drunkenness induced by hard liquor. It was the drunkenness, far more terrible, of mad, delirious excitement with an utterly reckless disregard for consequences. Like the panic of frightful fear, unreasoning, unexplainable, unrestrained.

Maddest and wildest of all was the Ace High, which appeared to attract the most reckless spirits. Dirk Hudson, his cut cheek plastered, his knuckles raw and bloody, paused for a word with Slade and Sime Bowman.

"Another night like this and I'll get out of the saloon business," he declared. "Three men have been shot in here tonight and one knifed, and it's not finished yet. This is the limit!"

He cast an envious glance at Sol Bajo, who was strolling past. "Nothing affects him," he growled. "Cold as ice water. Went out a while back to clear the smoke from his eyes and came back fresh as a daisy."

Hudson hurried off to quell a row starting on the dance floor. Sime Bowman shook his head and took a drink.

"I almost wonder if progress is worth the price we pay for it," he observed. "I've seen the elephant before, but never anything like this."

"It will pass," Slade said quietly. "Do you recall seeing a bad summer storm with black clouds and flashing lightning, and rolling thunder, and a deluge of rain that threatened to drown everything? Remember how bright and green and peaceful everything was after the storm had passed and the sun came out again. You wouldn't appreciate the sunshine and peace if it wasn't for the storms. Well, this thing is just like that. It's black and vicious and deadly, but after it will come the same growth and quickening of life as follows the storm. It will pass."

"Maybe," Bowman agreed doubtfully, "but it takes a sort

of strong faith to see good coming out of what's going on in this town tonight."

Gradually the screeching turmoil dimmed and subdued; tired nature was exacting its toll. Along the shadowy streets, weary men lurched and staggered in search of rest. The saloons were extinguishing their lights, casting out reluctant diehards who still persisted in their search for greater hilarity but were really too tired to put up much of an argument. Horses stood with drooping heads at the hitchracks. Their masters slept in the dust beside them. The kindly dark hid a man who fled in terror of his life. Somewhere a woman screamed like an enraged panther, and echoed the scream with shrill, hysterical laughter. A burst of curses was followed by the sodden thud of blows, then silence.

Death lay down the dark streets, and on whiskey-soaked sawdust, and in disordered, deserted tents. Here and there a lurid glow of light hinted at the dissolute license within. The roar of Pearson had changed to an incoherent mumble, a feeble yammering that gulped and retched to a ghastly stillness.

In the east the sky grayed, blushed rosy red, alchemized to gold. And in the first soft light of the dawn, Pearson lay motionless with a semblance of death accentuated by the sprawled forms that lay on disordered beds, in the dust of the street, in corners of darkened rooms. The sun rose in flame and gladness and the rangeland was a beauty that was an exquisite agony to look upon; but Pearson lay stark and hideous, exhausted and prostrate. Somewhere a bird sang a note of liquid melody. A lonesome little wind made music in the branches. The waters of the streams flashed back the sunlight in spears of silver. The hills stood robed in glory. But Pearson slept.

13

Despite the excitement of the night before and the late-
ness of the hour when he went to bed, Walt Slade was
awake before mid-morning. After a dip in the icy waters of
the big horse trough in the back of the stable, he headed for
the Ace High and breakfast. He walked with head erect, his
stride lithe and assured, in startling contrast to the shambling,
bleary-eyed individuals he met on the way.

The Ace High was scrubbed and shining when Slade
arrived there. Sol Bajo was on the job, looking little the
worse for his hectic night.

Sime Bowman was just sitting down at a table when Slade
entered. He glanced enviously at the tall Ranger.

"Don't know how you do it," he growled as he ordered a
cup of black coffee. "My mouth tastes like an old potato and
I got a head as big as an accordian, and my nerves were
so keyed up I couldn't sleep; but you look fresh as a yearling."

"Reckon I'm copper-lined," Slade replied cheerfully, giving
a waiter an order which included a big portion of ham and
eggs and apple pie to top it off with.

Bowman gulped and grew slightly green around the
mouth as the plate of ham and eggs was placed before The
Hawk. Slade chuckled and set himself to the meal with
the enthusiasm of a man who had known what it is to find
good food scarce.

"And look at Bajo!" complained Bowman. "*He* looks like
he'd just come from a church sociable. Hey, Sol, ain't you
been to bed at all?"

Bajo turned and regarded him with his inscrutable darkly
blue eyes, his handsome face expressionless.

"Not yet," he replied. "I sent Hudson to bed; he was all
in. But somebody had to straighten up this place so I stayed
on. Now I'm going to ride down to my ranch and sleep

twelve hours, that is as soon as I have a surrounding like Slade's got."

Bowman gave a hollow groan, gulped in his throat and ordered more black coffee. Slade's eyes were very thoughtful as Bajo headed for the kitchen.

He was thinking of Dirk Hudson's gashed face from which Doctor Cole had removed bits of broken glass.

Sol Bajo came back from the kitchen, paused at their table and glanced around.

"Well, everything appears to be in shape," he remarked. "I think I'll be riding."

"Dirk sure is lucky to have you, Sol," Bowman remarked. "You're sure a big help to him and he should appreciate all you do for him."

For the first time Slade saw Bajo show emotion. His eyes flashed and there was a queer, strained look on his face.

"I ask no favors from anyone," he said shortly. "I do my work and get paid for it. Strictly a business proposition." With a nod, he walked out.

"Now what set *him* off?" Bowman wondered. "Didn't seem to like what I said. Maybe things aren't so smooth between him and Dirk as they look to be."

"Some business difference, perhaps," Slade hazarded. "And after a night like the one he just went through, I wouldn't be surprised if his nerves are a bit on edge despite the control he exercises. It is almost a fetish with some men to show no emotion whatsoever, and they find any intimation that they should irritating. Often a psychological manifestation of the introvert."

Bowman jerked his shoulders resignedly. "There you go again, talking clean over my head," he declared. "You'd ought to sit down with Sol—he often uses the same sort of words you do. Maybe he just can't make Dirk understand what he's saying and gets worked up because of it."

"You don't consider Hudson an educated man?"

"I gather he never had much chance at school," Bowman returned. "I know Sol handles all his book work for him and usually does the talking when salesmen come around, and so on."

Bowman downed another cup of black coffee and lumbered

to his feet. "I'm going back to bed and see if I can't sleep a little," he announced. "I feel awful."

After the rancher departed, Slade sat on at the table for a while, drinking coffee, smoking and thinking. The mystery of Bone Canyon had abruptly developed a brand new angle. It was startlingly coincidental that Dirk Hudson should have had his face cut by flying glass at just about the time one of the Alhambra robbers went through a window head-first.

Of course Hudson's story of how he received his injury might well be authentic, but the parallel was distinctly interesting. Slade tried to recall what he had heard concerning the Ace High owner. Not much. Hudson was a reputable businessman, well thought of by his associates; that much was apparent. As to his antecedents, Slade knew nothing. As a man of affairs in the community and in touch with other businessmen, he could possibly be in a position to obtain information not readily available to the general public. That phase must be considered.

Not that Slade really suspected that Hudson was mixed up in the skullduggery going on. He had just been started thinking about the Ace High owner and, he admitted to himself, he was grasping at a straw. Anything out of the ordinary attracted his attention, and seeing that so far he had been unable to hit on a possible suspect, he did not intend to ignore even the slightest lead. As a result of his cogitations, he saddled Shadow and rode east through Bone Canyon, turning south on the Cooper trail.

When Slade reached Cooper, he went straight to the bank. The president greeted him warmly.

"You sure hit the nail on the head," he chuckled. "It was a fine piece of work, a fine piece of work! I don't hesitate to say that if the robbery had succeeded the bank would have found itself in a very embarrassing position. Our insurance premiums, if we could have gotten any more insurance, would have risen to the point of being crippling. A fine piece of work! Now what can I do for you?"

"I would like to see a list of the bank's stockholders," Slade told him.

The president called a clerk and the list was quickly procured. Slade studied it intently. Most of the names meant nothing to him, three stood out—Wesley Harlow, Robert

Higgins and Dirk Hudson. He laid the list down and raised his eyes to the president.

"Did Harlow, Higgins and Hudson know of the methods that were to be employed in sending the latest payroll money and the Gonzales payroll to Pearson?" he asked.

"Harlow and Higgins knew," the president replied. "The matter was discussed at a director's meeting. Hudson did not, so far as I know. He seems to be a steady young man and invests his money wisely; but he is not a director and was not present at the meeting."

"I see," Slade said thoughtfully; "but Higgins and Harlow were."

"That's right," said the president, "but surely you don't suspect any of those men of being in complicity with the robbers?"

"I suspect nobody in particular and everybody in general," Slade replied. "I am endeavoring to ascertain where a possible leak might have occurred. You know folks sometimes talk out of turn, and when the wrong pair of ears is listening."

"That is so," the president admitted.

"As the situation stands, somebody undoubtedly let slip information that enabled the outlaws to learn just how and when the Gonzales money was to be shipped," Slade pointed out. "They guessed correctly again when they tried to hold up the stage yesterday. As I said before, it was not beyond the realm of possibility that they would see through your strategem of the two guarded coaches. That might be the answer. But, considering the Gonzales incident, there is also the chance that somebody let something slip. Are any of the other directors in business in or around Pearson?"

The banker shook his head. "Jim Green owns the ranch just southeast of Harlow's holdings, but I don't think he ever even visits Pearson. The others are Cooper residents."

"Which, I would say, rules them out," Slade said. "I am of the opinion that whatever happened took place in Pearson."

"Sort of narrows it down to Harlow and Higgins, eh?"

"Sort of," Slade conceded noncommittally.

As Slade rode back to Pearson he did some very hard thinking. He appeared to be continually running up against a blank wall. If Dirk Hudson was his logical suspect, what did he have on Hudson? Absolutely nothing. Hudson had not even been at the director's meeting when the plans for frustrating the outlaws were discussed. Of course he was a business associate of Bob Higgins, and Higgins had mentioned that with Hudson, among others, he discussed business matters. Knowing Hudson to be a stockholder in the bank, it was not beyond the realm of possibility that he had revealed the plans to Hudson. It would not have been hard for an adroit man, by a little subtle probing, circumstances being what they were, to get Higgins to talk.

All pure conjecture, of course, with nothing really substantial to back it up, but so far it was all he had to go on.

He reflected uneasily that he might be doing Dirk Hudson a grave injustice, but salved his conscience with the determination not to do anything without absolute proof of his guilt that could possibly harm Hudson.

All in all, he was in very much of a baffled mood and felt he had learned nothing tangible. Somewhere there was a mastermind directing the outlaw activities in the section and one who was an expert at keeping under cover. But such an individual must to a large extent rely on subordinates to carry out his plans, and there Slade hoped to get a break. Sooner or later somebody would make a slip.

It was well past dark when he reached Pearson. After seeing that all of Shadow's wants were provided for, he dropped in at the Ace High for something to eat.

Dirk Hudson was back on the job; he paused at Slade's table.

"Well, how do you feel now?" the Ranger asked.

"Physically, okay, but I've got a mental and moral hangover," Hudson replied morosely. "I meant what I said last night—one more such night and I'm out of the saloon business. In fact, I'm seriously considering getting out, anyhow. I can't help but feel that I am to a certain extent responsible for the things that happened here. It's the stuff sold on my side of the bar that makes the trouble on this side. All right to say that if I don't sell it, somebody else will, but that doesn't relieve me of responsibility. I'm making money, all right, but money isn't everything, although I've known what it is to be without any, and that isn't pleasant, either. But I've been investing what I make in legitimate enterprises. No, I didn't have it so easy when I was young. Dad was a squaw man. Mom was the daughter of Kepnau, the Comanche war chief."

"I've heard of him," Slade interpolated. "Captain Hays spoke very highly of him. He said if all the chiefs were like Kepnau, the whites and the Comanches would have gotten along, settled their differences and lived together in peace."

"Yes, Kepnau was a fine man," nodded Hudson. "His wife, Mom's mother, was a Mexican girl he carried off in the course of one of the Comanche raids into Mexico during what they called the 'Mexican Moon.'

"Not that there was much need of 'carrying' her off," he added with a chuckle. "She was a beauty and Kepnau was one of the handsomest men, white or red, I ever saw; it had all the appearances of a true love match. But just the same Dad was rated a squaw man and Mom an Indian girl, which didn't make things any easier for me."

"It would appear you've come a long way and deserve a good deal of credit," Slade observed.

"Oh, not so much," Hudson deprecated. "Opportunity sort of dropped in my lap, as it were. I believed in the gold strike when most folks didn't think it would amount to much, and got in on the ground floor. I bought some bank stock when the figure quoted was much lower than it is today, and some Gonzales Mine stock when it could be had for very little. Yes, I've been doing all right and I'm about ready to buy a spread and settle down to raising sows. That's what I was cut out for, I feel. My first real job was one of riding. Tackled a few other things, like mining, dealing cards, working behind the bar and so on, but I've always had a hankering to get into the cattle business. That's why I've done a lot of things to get money together," he added, with an enigmatic smile. "Be seeing you."

Slade watched him saunter away and shook his head as he turned his attention to his food. If Hudson was putting on an act he was putting on a good one. His voice had the ring of sincerity. Slade gave a disgusted mutter, downed a cup of coffee scalding hot and made a remark or two appropriate to the occasion and not altogether directed at the hot coffee. He appeared to be getting nowhere fast. Hudson might be sincere, and then again he might be doing an excellent job of covering up. Slade had already been of the opinion that Hudson had Indian blood and now the saloon-keeper had explained that in a manner hard to argue with. Old Kepnau's grandson? He could very well be; Kepnau had several daughters and marriage between the whites and the Comanches was not so uncommon despite the Texas boast that it was not a squaw man state.

And if Hudson was beginning to feel that things were getting a bit too hot for comfort, admitting he was really mixed up in something, and was planning to pull out, he had adroitly laid the groundwork of a logical explanation for so doing. Slade finished his dinner and went to bed.

14

Slade was up early the following morning. After breakfast, he strolled along the main street. He was directly opposite Doctor Cole's office when a man wearing rangeland clothes tore into town on a lathered horse, pulled the animal to a sliding halt in front of the doctor's office and bounded up the two steps to the front door. His eyes were wild and he breathed almost as hard as did the blowing horse. Slade instantly crossed the street and entered the office.

"Arn Bowman," he heard the cowhand gulp. "Shot some time last night—dusted both sides of his shirt—we found him a little while ago."

"Take it easy, take it easy, and give me the lowdown on what shape he's in," counselled the doctor. "Hello, Slade, come in."

"He's in mighty bad shape," the cowboy replied, growing calmer. "Ain't hardly breathing at all and you almost can't feel his heart beat. May be dead by now. Sime's with him. I got here fast as I could."

"Bullet went clean through him?"

"That's right, dusted both sides of his shirt. Went in just above his heart I think and come out his back."

"Sounds bad," muttered the doctor. "Heart's liable to give out before I get there. I'll hitch up and make it as fast as I can."

"Doc," Slade interrupted, "give me a heart stimulant and a hypodermic and what else you figure I'll need and I'll get there on Shadow in half the time you'll take. I know how to administer the drug and I'll do what I can till you get there. It may be a chance to save him."

The doctor shot him a keen glance. "Okay," he said. "You can't do more'n kill him, and it looks like he'll probably die before I get there, anyway. Here's a needle and compresses, antiseptics and bandage. And here's nitroglycerin. Don't

94

forget, now, the dosage is a hundredth of a grain. Give him more and if it's a wind wound—the lung perforated—and he's bleeding internally, you *will* kill him. Understand?"

"Yes, I understand. I've handled such cases before," Slade replied as he pocketed what the doctor handed him and hurried from the office. Scant minutes later he was riding east through Bone Canyon, steadily increasing Shadow's pace.

"It's up to you, horse," he told the great black. "Give me all you've got and maybe we'll make it."

Shadow responded nobly. He snorted, slugged his head above the bit. His glorious black mane tossed and rippled in the wind of his passing as he literally poured his long body over the ground. Soon he was traveling at top speed which Slade knew would not slacken till the goal was reached.

Slade's heart was filled with anxiety. Many a time Shadow had pitted his speed, strength and endurance against fleshly rivals, and had always won. But this was different; now he was racing the grim arch-enemy of mankind, whose tireless stride neither storm nor night nor glare of sun can stay. The cowboy's report had been far from encouraging. Slade had seen such symptoms before and they generally meant a steady draining-away of strength until the struggling heart ceased to respond to the urge to live. Who could have shot the young rancher? he wondered. Had he come upon wide-loopers or other outlaws? Or had an unseen enemy again struck from ambush? He'd had no time to ask questions. Well, he'd find out. More than fifteen miles to cover! Shadow was giving his all, but would it be enough? Slade settled himself in the saddle and encouraged the flying horse with voice and hand.

They flashed out of the canyon, past the Cooper trail, down the long slope where Arn had been chased by the Bradded H cowhands, and swerved into the trail that slanted southeast.

"Just a little more, horse," he pleaded, "just a little more!"

Shadow snorted reply and managed to increase his gait a little.

A small ranchhouse set on a knoll and surrounded by piñons came into view. Slade knew it must be Sol Bajo's horse-ranch *casa;* the next would be Bowman's lazy B. About four miles yet to go, he estimated. Shadow's hoofs drummed the surface of the trail. They were passing over rolling rangeland now but ahead loomed low hills thickly brush grown, Bowman's goat pastures.

They reached the hills, fled past them and were again on grassland. Ten minutes more and Slade sighted the Lazy B ranchhouse, a large and comfortable-looking building set back a little ways from the trail. He halted Shadow and mounted the steps to the veranda. Sime Bowman opened the door.

"My God, Slade, I'm glad to see you!" he exclaimed. "Maybe you can do something for the poor kid; I'm afraid he's about gone."

He led Slade to where the wounded man lay on a couch. Slade bent over him.

Young Arn's breathing was barely perceptible, his pulse a feeble flutter. Slade wasted no time.

"Boiling water,". he said, "get it going fast."

"There's some on the stove right now," Bowman answered and conducted Slade to the kitchen where a scared-looking cook was stoking the fire.

"Figured the doctor would need some and got it going," Bowman explained.

Slade went to work with smooth efficiency. He sterilized the hypodermic, measured with the greatest care the infinitesimal dose of the heart stimulant that a slip could render fatal. He charged the syringe and returned to the room where Arn Bowman lay. He swiftly applied the antiseptic solution and injected the drug. Then he turned his attention to the wound. Wounds, rather. Arn had a bullet gash in his left thigh and the skin just above his left temple had been cut by a slug.

What concerned Slade, however, was the blue hole in his left breast. Thankfully he saw that there were no blood bubbles rising; evidently the lung was untouched. There was a slight slow seepage of blood. He proceeded to cleanse and pad the wound, and the perforation where the bullet had emerged from Bowman's back. Then he gave attention to the flesh wound in the thigh and the slight head wound.

"Slug evidently missed the aorta and other large blood vessels," he told Sime Bowman. "That's all I can do."

He felt the wounded man's pulse and nodded with satisfaction. "Picking up a little," he said. "Believe he'll hold out till the doctor gets here, at least."

Several of the Lazy B hands were standing silently in the room. Slade drew Sime aside.

"Now tell me what happened," he said.

"He rode up to the north pasture before daylight, close to where the fence separates our holding from Sol Bajo's, to check some goats for shearing before they scattered to feed. Been doing that for the last few days," Bowman explained. "Luckily a couple of the boys rode up there right after breakfast and found him lying not far this side of the fence."

"Confound it! I told you not to ride alone," Slade said irritably.

"Why, I haven't been, but I didn't think they were after Arn, too," Sime protested.

"Well, you thought wrong," Slade retorted. "But I guess I'm as much to blame as you. I should have specifically mentioned Arn in my warning. I thought you'd understand I meant both of you, and that's where *I* thought wrong."

He returned to the patient. Arn's breathing appeared a bit more regular, his pulse a little stronger.

"I believe he'll make it," Slade said with satisfaction. "Nothing to do now but wait for the doctor."

"Come on out to the kitchen and have some coffee," Sime suggested.

"I will," Slade accepted the invitation. "Feel that I need it."

"No use trying to thank you for what you did," Sime said, his voice shaking a little. "I've a notion you saved Arn's life."

"Hope so," Slade answered, "we'll have to wait and see."

"You seem to make a business of saving us," Sime added.

Nearly an hour elapsed before the doctor's buggy pulled up in front of the ranchhouse. The old practitioner gave the patient a swift examination, nodded to Slade.

"Saved his life, I'd say," he reported. "Very likely have been dead before I got here. It's bad, but he's young and tough as a pine knot. I figure he'll pull through."

Sime Bowman gave a great sigh of relief and his eyes were a trifle misty as they rested on El Halcon.

"Doc," Slade said, "wouldn't you say the bullet that struck him in the breast ranged upward?"

"It did, and that's very likely what kept it from killing him right off," the doctor replied.

"Which would indicate that the shot was fired from a man on the ground, Arn being on horseback."

"So I'd presume," said the doctor.

"But the one that struck his thigh ranged downward," Slade observed.

"Right again," agreed Cole.

"Looks like he was lying on the ground when the shot which struck his thigh was fired," Slade remarked reflectively.

"And the one that nicked his scalp, also," added the doctor. "Not much doubt about that, I'd say."

"Hellion wanted to be sure and do a finish job, eh?" growled Sime.

"Looks that way," Slade agreed. "Doc, that wound in his breast was made by a fairly small calibre gun, was it not?"

"That's my opinion," nodded the doctor.

"A thirty-thirty, I'd say," Slade remarked musingly. "Not exactly a common calibre for these parts, but you do see one now and then. Carries a long ways and packs a punch, but lacks the shocking power of a forty-four or forty-five. That's where Arn was lucky, too. A big calibre slug would very likely have torn his whole side out. How long do you think it will be, Doc, before he recovers consciousness?"

"Ten or twelve hours; the drugs have taken effect and he's drifted into a natural sleep, which is the very best thing for him. He'll be weak when he rouses up but, I predict, on the mend."

"Are you going to stay with him?"

"Of course, until he regains consciousness, longer if necessary, though I doubt if it will be. If you're riding to town, Slade, spread the word around where I am, in case an emergency arises."

"I'll do that," Slade promised. "Yes, I'm riding to town; no use for me to hang around here longer. But I'd like to see the spot where Arn was picked up."

"Buck will show you," Sime said. "He was one of the fellers who found him."

"That'll be fine," Slade answered. "I'm ready to ride whenever you are, Buck."

"Be with you in a jiffy," replied the lanky puncher Sime designated.

Five minutes later he and Slade were riding north across the range. Slade noticed plenty of cows wearing the Lazy B burn, good stock and in prime condition. Sime Bowman knew the cattle business, all right.

For some time they traveled the grassland, then gradually worked into the low hills to the north. This was broken country and thickly grown with brush. Here they encountered the goats browsing on the leaves and berries and pausing to regard them with mild, questioning eyes.

"Funny little devils," observed Buck. "But they're easy to handle and you get to sort of liking them. They're different from sheep. Sheep are all alike and you can't tell one bleatin' critter from another, but goats got personality. You soon get to recognize one from the others."

Finally they reached a wide, open space through which a little stream that had its source in a big spring flowed. In the distance strands of barbed wire gleamed dully.

"Here's where we found him," said Buck. "Right up there close to the fence. Was layin' sprawled out with his horse standing beside him."

Slade studied the terrain. It was open ground on both sides of the wire for quite a ways. North of the wire, however, thick growth began.

"Sidewinder must have been holed up over there the other side of the wire," he remarked. "The only place where he could find cover."

He estimated the distance with his eye. "Good shooting," he observed. "More than two hundred yards. No wonder he didn't more than nick him after he was on the ground."

"I'd like to get a change to nick *him!*" growled Buck. "The ornery son of a hydrophobia skunk! You feel sure it wasn't one of the Harlow bunch, Slade?"

"I'm positive," Slade replied.

"Sime 'pears to agree with you," Buck admitted. "He says he just can't figure Wes Harlow doing such a thing. Maybe he's right, but maybe one of Harlow's hands got off the reservation."

"Possible, but highly unlikely, in my estimation," Slade replied. "Right here he was lying, you say?"

"That's right," answered Buck. "Right here on the grass."

For some moments, Slade sat studying the bristle of growth north of the wire. Beyond it were the crests of rises and farther on, he knew, the hills petered out. Very likely somebody had watched from one of the rises, had probably noted Arn Bowman's habit of riding north in the early hours and had availed himself of the opportunity to do a chore of drygulching.

Buck was glancing around the clearing. "The goats, a lot of them, huddle up here in the night," he remarked. "Come here for the water, I reckon. Never seem to drink in the daytime, only at night, so far as I've seen."

Slade nodded absently, his eyes still on the belt of chaparral.

"I think I'll give that brush a once-over," he told Buck. "Might be able to learn something."

"Okay," said Buck, "we'll let down the wire."

"Won't be necessary," Slade smiled. He pointed Shadow's nose toward the fence; his voice rang out, "Take it, feller!"

Shadow "took it," soaring over the wire with a foot to spare. Buck let out an astounded yelp,

"Good gosh, feller! That's some critter you've got!"

"He'll do," Slade replied. "Now I want you to sit your horse right where you picked up Arn's body."

Buck moved his mount to the designed position; Slade rode on to the bristle of growth. At its edge he reined in and dismounted. Gazing back toward Buck, he moved a few paces to the left.

"I figure this should be about in line," he told Shadow. "Go ahead and down a little grass; I'll be with you shortly."

Leaving Shadow contentedly cropping, he entered the chaparral. Back and forth he ranged through its ragged fringe. It was some little time before he discovered what he sought. Lying on the ground beside a thick bush were three brass cartridge cases. As he expected they would be, they were thirty-thirty calibre. He turned them over in his fingers, then slipped them into his pocket and continued his investigation.

In the soft earth outside the growth were the prints of boot heels scored deep as the drygulcher set himself solidly for the shot. Slade made out where he turned and walked away into the bush. A broken twig here and there, a few leaves stripped from a branch were enough for the keen eyes of El Halcon. The signs led through the growth for nearly a hundred yards, ending at a track, little more than a game trail, that wound east and west through the chaparral. Slade studied its surface and spotted the prints of a horse, headed west. And west would be toward the main trail which led from the Bowman ranch to Bone Canyon and town.

"Chances are the hellion covered his tracks on the trail," Slade muttered. "Mixed them up with other prints so there'd be no telling which way he went. Might be able to pick up his trail, though. Worth trying, anyhow."

He retraced his steps to where he had left Shadow and continued to the fence where Buck waited.

"There's a track in there that appears to lead to the trail," he told the cowboy. "So I might just as well take it. Yes, I found where the devil holed up and the three empty shells he ejected from his gun as he fired. Yes, thirty-thirties. Mention that to Doc Cooper when you get back to the ranchhouse. Tell Bowman I expect to ride down to-morrow or the next day. Be seeing you."

"Okay," Buck replied. "Be seeing you."

Slade returned to Shadow and led him through the growth to the track. There he mounted and rode west at fair speed. He studied the growth intently as he rode but there was no sign of life apparent other than the contented twittering and fluttering of birds. He quickened Shadow's gait a little.

It was gloomy under the growth for the branches interlaced above and let very little sunshine filter through. So gloomy that Slade, his attention centered on the dark chaparral on either side, did not see the thin, strong rope stretched tightly across the track at knee height.

Nor did Shadow see it. He hit it in full stride and went down in a sprawling heap, pitching the unprepared Ranger over his head like a stone from a sling. Slade hit the ground with great force. A blaze of intense light stormed before his eyes, then wave on wave of blackness—and oblivion.

15

OUT OF THE GROWTH dashed three men. One, tall, broad-shouldered wore a black handkerchief swathed over his face and pierced with eyeholes. The others, squat and brawny, were unmasked. They hurled themselves on the prostrate Ranger and swiftly bound his hands behind his back.

"Plumb knocked out," said the tall man. "He'll be coming to after a bit, however, to wish he hadn't. All right, catch the horse."

One of the squat men approached Shadow, who had regained his feet and stood blowing and snorting. The man reached for the bridle. There was a gleam of teeth, a vicious lunge and the man leaped back with a gutteral yelp of pain, blood streaming from his gashed arm. Shadow dashed into the growth and disappeared.

"To the devil with the brute, let him go," the tall man called to the other, who was wringing his blood-dripping fingers and cursing in several languages. "Come on, you're not hurt—just a scratch. Come on, I say, before you have something to really yell about." He turned to the other squat man who was standing beside Slade and regarding his injured companion with solid indifference.

"Your horse will pack double," he said. "Bring the critters out of the brush and then get up behind the crupper and hold onto him."

The other obeyed. The masked man lifted the unconscious Ranger's heavy form, apparently with ease, and boosted him into the saddle.

"Ease him down to the bronc's neck while I fasten his legs to the stirrup straps," he ordered. "That's right. Hang onto him and don't let him slip sideways. Here's the bridle."

"Fork your bronc," he told the second man, who was still

mumbling and muttering and cherishing his injured arm.
"Let's go!"

He mounted his own horse as he spoke. The cavalcade got
under way, heading east along the shadowy track. Mile after
mile they rode, Slade swaying and reeling in the saddle, his
face buried in the horse's coarse mane, the man behind the
crupper steadying his flaccid form and managing his mount
with one hand.

The country began to change, the hills dwindling to rises
that also soon ceased. They were on grassland now, but
directly ahead, to the southeast, was a wide stretch of arid
soil of a desert-like nature.

Before they reached the wasteland, Slade recovered consciousness. It was a gradual and painful process and it was
some time before he realized where he was. Memory flooded
back, and with it the decision to stimulate unconsciousness
for a little while longer. His teeth tightened together in
bitter anger, largely directed at himself. He had obligingly
ridden into a trap laid for him. Doubtless somebody had
seen him riding to the Lazy B ranchhouse and had shrewdly
anticipated his subsequent movements. He had been watched
from one of the hill crests and when he decided to follow
the track to the main trail, whoever had been watching
had circled ahead and made preparations for his downfall
actually and figuratively, and he had blithely cooperated to
the fullest extent. But why the devil, he wondered, didn't
they kill him at once instead of bearing him off a captive.
The answer to that wasn't long in coming, and it was not a
pleasant answer. Very likely no such quick and merciful fate
was in store for him. His face was lying sideways on the
horse's neck and through slitted eyes he stole a glance at the
man riding on his right, and felt cold all over.

There was no mistaking that broad, dark and ferocious
countenance; the man was an Apache Indian. It was logical
to assume that the one riding back of the crupper and holding him in position in the saddle was also an Apache. In
front another man was riding, but Slade could no more than
get a glimpse of his back.

His captors rode in silence; they covered another mile and
did not speak a word. Slade felt his strained position becoming unbearable and decided there was no sense in keeping up the pretense further. He rolled his head, groaned,

jerked and twitched, simulating returning consciousness. He gradually straightened up and gazed about dazedly.

The man riding in front turned his head and Slade saw that he was masked. He spoke, his voice muffled behind the black cloth and, Slade was pretty sure, deliberately disguised.

"Take it easy and don't start anything or you'll get a knock that will put you out again," he advised and faced back to the front.

Slade did not answer, but he heeded the warning. He was weak and sick and his head ached abominably, in no condition to put up a struggle of any kind at the moment. He would have to let events shape their course and be prepared to take advantage of any opportunity. Strength was slowly flowing back into his cramped limbs but he was careful not to show it, sagging against the arm that held him in the saddle, lurching and wobbling.

He glanced at the dark hand grasping the bridle of the horse on his right. Blood oozed from a jagged tear just above the wrist, a cut that Slade quickly catalogued as having been made by slashing teeth. With satisfaction he realized that Shadow had apparently escaped. The faithful animal would follow him, keeping out of sight the while, that he well knew. Not that he would likely be of any help, but it would be comforting to know he was near.

Slade studied the man riding in front. That he was no Apache he was pretty well convinced. He was tall and well formed, with broad shoulders, totally unlike the squat figure on his right, and, presumably, the one mounted behind him. At any rate, his build hinted at white blood. He raised his hand to adjust the mask and its coloring corroborated the Ranger's deduction. It was bronzed by sun and wind but quite different in hue from the dark hand that gripped the bridle of his own mount.

Directly ahead was the stretch of desert. They rode onto the sands and straight ahead, apparently steering for a belt of gray and dusty-looking growth a mile or so distant. The sun was slanting westward, but out on the arid sands the heat was still terrific. Slade began to perspire and his mouth felt like the inside of an oven.

Within a hundred yards of the straggle of growth, which Slade could see extended westward for a long distance, gradually drawing near the southern terminus of the hills that encroached on the rangeland, the tall leader swerved his horse to ride parallel to the chaparral and slowed his pace. His eyes, through holes in his mask, appeared to be searching the ground. Finally, with an exclamation of satisfaction, he pulled up.

"Get him out of the hull," he ordered his companions. He turned his bleak gaze on Slade, his eyes dark through the holes in the black cloth.

"Try to put up a fight and I'll gut-shoot you and leave you to die sweating," he promised as the others cut the lashing that secured Slade's legs to the stirrup straps and performed a like office for his bound wrists.

Slade let his arms fall to his sides, rejoicing in the relief afforded by the removal of the cords. He offered no resistance as he was hauled from the saddle and hurled to the ground. His arms were stretched out at right angles to his body and held by the two Apaches.

The tall man dismounted. From his saddle pouches he took four sharpened stakes and a heavy billet of wood. He proceeded to drive a stake into the ground beside each of the captive's wrists. Another moment and the wrists were lashed to the stakes, giving them little play. Slade's ankles received similar treatment. The masked man straightened up and gazed down at the helpless prisoner. Abruptly he turned his glance to one of the Apaches.

"Put those guns down beside his hands, where he can see them but out of reach," he ordered. "No, you can't keep them," as the other gutteraled protest. "Those guns are distinctive and might be recognized. And getting caught packing a dead Ranger's guns is a sure way to stretch rope. Put them down, I say. That's right. Let him look at them and long for them, a little later. He'd be mighty glad of a chance to put a slug through his own head before long."

He turned his gaze back to Slade, regarded him in silence for a long moment, shrugged his broad shoulders.

"Well, *adios, Señor* Ranger," he said, a jeering note creeping into his voice. "I trust you will sleep well. But not for long, not for long! And before it's realized that you are out of the picture for good and another meddler sent here, I will have finished my business in this section and will have departed, with nobody even suspecting the part I played here. And the long-dead will at last know peace."

With the melodramatic and cryptic statement, he swung into his saddle, motioned his silent followers to do likewise and rode west without turning his head, his ferocious-faced henchmen trailing behind.

Twisting his head sideways, Slade watched the evil trio dim into the distance. He turned his attention to his own predicament, which was horrifying in the extreme. He was already suffering severely from thirst and the hot sands and the blazing sun seemed to be drying the blood in his veins. The sun was well down the western sky and soon it would be cooler, but that would be but a temporary lessening of his torment. He was strong and would undoubtedly live through the night and through the following long day of hideous torture.

His glance dropped to the big blue gun lying less than a foot from his emprisoned wrist and he understood to the full the fiendish ingenuity of the man who had doomed him to a death of agony. Soon indeed he would long for the swift end to his suffering the weapon would provide. Almost within hand's reach! But it might as well be a thousand miles distant. His mind would dwell on the arm, dwell with an intensity that would mount and mount until he would be a gibbering maniac, struggling and screaming, moaning prayers to the unheeding heavens. Already he was afflicted by a mental shivering that threatened to topple the throne of his reason. And this was nothing to what was to come. He tugged at the rawhide thongs that bound his wrists to the stakes, but it was impossible to bring any appreciable amount of his strength to bear, and the pegs were driven firmly into the ground. Not a chance in the world of loosening them.

The effort increased his thirst and he gave over the attempt, gasping for breath. His body relaxed and he lay staring up at the hot sky.

Suddenly he felt a sharp little pain in his left hand. He craned his neck to discover the author of the unexpected pang. Perched on his palm was a large black ant. He twitched his hand petulantly to dislodge the creature, but almost instantly another took its place and was joined by still another. Again the little fiery twinge, and again. Slade swore angrily and jerked his pinioned wrist. He turned his head sideways and went rigid, staring with dilated eyes.

From the direction of the thicket a thin black stream was flowing toward him, and abruptly he realized the full horror of his position. He had been pegged out close to an ant hill and the voracious little demons scented food!

A wave of near panic swept over him. Once he had seen a man who had been pegged out beside an ant hill. Or, rather, the awful caricature of what had been a man—lipless, noseless, cheekless, a grinning death's head with feebly champing jaws and whistling breath. And as Slade had stared in horror, an ant scurryed into one eyeless socket and out the other!

And the man still lived!

16

THE UNREASONING PANIC of sheer terror surged over Slade like the waves of the Atlantic over a lost continent. And no wonder! Such a doom as he faced was enough to affright the bravest. Only the mindless would not know fear under such circumstances. He struggled madly, arching his body, tugging and straining until the blood from his lacerated wrists stained the rawhide thongs. Only sheer exhaustion caused him to desist. With a mighty effort of will he got a grip on himself. He rolled his head from side to side to dislodge the ants that were now swarming over him, switched his hands, beat the sands with his feet. His body was a fiery agony as the formic acid injected with each tiny bite coursed through his blood stream. But he forced his mind to dwell sanely on his predicament in a frantic effort to discover some means of escape. In black despair, he admitted there was none. All he could do was pray for death to put an end to his torment.

But the urge to live was still strong and he continued to fight to keep the black devils from his eyes and mouth. So far he had succeeded fairly well despite the burning torture of the bites on his hands, arms and body. He concentrated on the vital sector and endured the excruciating pain that threatened to drive him to raging insanity. He wondered dimly how much suffering the human frame could absorb before the crucified flesh could no longer feel. Was this fiery rack something that could continue without end? The vision of the man whose cleanly gnawed bones gleamed white and who still could express his awful woe danced before his eyes. The shudder that shook him was cold beneath the burning winding sheet of pain.

A sound pierced the fog of near-delirium that enveloped

him. It was a familiar sound but seemingly out of accord with the circumstances. He tried to concentrate on it, to coordinate it with existing conditions.

Again it came, the unmistakable plaintive whinny of a horse. Slade shook the ants from his face, craned his neck and glared about. Shadow was standing at the edge of the chaparral, his ears pricked forward, gazing inquiringly at his master. Evidently he had circled through the growth to reach the spot.

Shadow! Maybe he could help somehow. Slade hadn't the slightest notion how he possibly could, but even the faintest glimmer of hope was something. He pursed his puffed lips and managed to whistle. Shadow snorted response and trotted forward until he was beside Slade. He stretched his head down and nuzzled the Ranger's hand, jerked back as an ant stung him on the nose. With an angry snort he reached down again and blew prodigiously through his nostrils, scattering ants in every direction. Slade scratched his nose, managed to clumsily pat it. Shadow snorted and blew again, stamping his feet nervously as the ants swarmed toward him. He knew something was very much wrong. Why didn't his master get up from there and brush off the swarming insects? Slade could read the question in his intelligent eyes.

The split reins were trailing. Shadow petulantly jerked his head and one of the stout straps slapped Slade across the face, slipped down and dangled beside his right hand. An inspiration came, and the dawn of hope. He began to talk to the horse, soothingly, gently. Ignoring the waves of pain that were flowing through limbs that no longer seemed to be his own.

"Down, feller, down," he pleaded, snapping his fingers.

Shadow lowered his head, suspiciously eyeing the ants that were scurrying all around. Slade managed to get the dangling rein between his fingers. Shadow raised his head and Slade began to clumsily and laboriously wind the strap around his hand, wriggling it back until it was behind his thumb and a couple of loops were around his wrist. He shuffled two more turns about his hand, gripped them tightly. Now would come the test.

"Trail, feller, trail! Easy, easy!" he gasped.

Shadow obediently started to move away, but the single strap pulled the bit hard against the side of his mouth and it was evidently painful. He stopped, blowing inquiringly. He'd never been asked to move in such a position before.

Slade's voice rose, urgent, compelling, a hoarse croak that quivered in his throbbing throat—"Trail, Shadow, trail!"

Again the big black began to move away. The strap tightened. The pressure on Slade's hand and wrist was almost unbearable, dwarfing even the torture of the stinging ants. The bones ground together and he feared that a little more would fracture the wrist. But he had to take it, no matter what happened. It was his last slim chance to escape death by unbelievable torture. His voice rang harshly, "Trail!"

Shadow lunged forward. The stab of agony through Slade's wrist and hand nearly caused him to faint; but the stake was loosening in the ground. He spoke again, "Trail!"

Once more the numbing pain that dewed his face with sweat as Shadow lunged harder than before. The rawhide thongs cut deeply into his flesh. Another hard jerk and the stake flew from the ground!

"Hold it!" Slade gasped. He writhed his body sideways, reached across and gripped the stake which prisoned his left wrist. A mighty tug and a wrench, a hard sideways pull and both hands were free. He struggled to a sitting position and freeing his ankles was absurdly easy. Gasping and panting, the stakes dangling from the thongs, he lurched to his feet, fell headlong, scrambled erect again. He reeled and staggered away from the swarming mass of ants to where Shadow stood. Leaning against the horse's barrel he freed his wrists of the stakes and then his ankles. He tore off his clothes and shook them clean of the clinging insects, stamping them into the ground with joyous abandon. His body was one vast fiery itch, but not even that could detract from the exultant thrill that coursed through his veins. He struggled back into his clothes, stumbled to where his guns lay, kicking ants right and left, picked them up and holstered them. Then he walked back to Shadow, who had moved farther from the anthill. The voracious devils streamed after him, but he paid them no heed. After a couple of ineffectual attempts he managed to swing into the saddle. His legs were still numb, his right wrist viciously sore and swelling but apparently had taken no serious hurt. With a last glance at the seething mass of baffled insects, he rode north by west. He had to find water soon. His lips were cracked and bleeding, his tongue swollen and blackened. He recalled that on the trip to the desert they had splashed through a shallow stream only a mile or so distant. After what seemed an eternity of torture, he saw its silvery gleam. He flopped from the saddle on the creek bank, flipped the bit from Shadow's mouth and then stretched out on the grass and drank and drank. Never, he thought, had he tasted anything so wonderful as that long draught of water. Greatly refreshed, he sat up, fished out the makings and clumsily rolled a cigarette. He was still in great pain but his strength was returning and he did not believe that his body had absorbed enough of the formic acid to be seriously affected.

He smoked the cigarette slowly, down to a short stub, pinched it out and had another long drink. Replacing the bit in Shadow's mouth, he tightened the cinches a little and mounted, this time without difficulty. He loosed his guns in their sheaths, made sure his Winchester was working smoothly in the saddle boot. He had little fear of meeting his late captors, but ardently hoped he would. To shoot it out with the friends would be a pleasure. For once in his life he experienced the seething urge for vengeance.

The sun sank in a glory of scarlet and gold. The twilight hush fell over the rangeland. Slade rode on through the deepening dusk, and under the star-burned sky of the night. Strange thoughts coursed through his mind and he knew he was a bit lightheaded from his sufferings and the poison in his blood. The ferocious faces of the two Apaches swam before his eyes, and the tall form of the masked leader. The ghost of Cocha rode the hills again, the old Mexican *pastor* had declared. Could such things be? Reason and experience said no, but—"There are more things in heaven and earth, Horatio, than are dreamt of in your philosophy."

Slade laughed aloud at his own conceit. He was a bit loco, no doubt about it. Cocha was dead, and he'd stay dead, but—

This time he swore, and quickened Shadow's pace a little. What he needed most was a bed, and some sleep to sweep the cobwebs from his brain.

The long slant to the northwest finally brought him to the trail only a few miles below the mouth of Bone Canyon; but it was well past midnight before he reached Pearson. He was in need of food but didn't feel up to the effort of obtaining it. After making sure Shadow was properly cared for, he tumbled into bed and despite his physical sufferings, which were still severe, he almost instantly sank into the sodden sleep of sheer exhaustion.

17

WHEN SLADE AWOKE, a gradual and somewhat painful process, the sunlight was slanting into the room from the west, and he knew he had slept for more than twelve hours. For a while he lay quiet, his mind gradually clearing, and conned over the recent hectic events. There were several vital points that demanded serious consideration.

First, he had been recognized as a Ranger, doubtless from the very start. Secondly, the tall masked man had intimated that he had just about one more important chore on hand before he pulled out, which would be soon. Slade cudgeled his brains in a desperate effort to surmise just what the cunning and utterly callous devil had in mind. Undoubtedly it was something big, and something that, as he said, would finish up his business in the section. It was up to him, Slade, to anticipate his intention and thwart him. But how? That was one devil of a question to answer when he had no idea where to look or what move to make. Well, as he had resolved before, he could only let events shape their own course and take advantage of any opportunity that offered. Yesterday Shadow had been the "opportunity," without which there would have been no today so far as Walt Slade was concerned. He got out of bed and began dressing. He was still in some pain and stiff and sore all over, and he knew he was slightly feverish. Which was to be expected and gave him no particular concern. The effects of the poison acid would gradually wear off. His right wrist was still much swollen and painful to move, but time would also take care of that.

All in all, he was considerably below standard, but he was fervently thankful that he was alive and not a fleshless skeleton lying out there on the hot sands. He went downstairs, pausing to rub Shadow's nose and stroke his glossy neck.

"If it wasn't for you, feller, I sure *wouldn't* be here,"

113

he told the horse who craned his neck and thrust his velvety muzzle into his hand. "You did it, feller. Not the first time you've pulled me out of a bad scrape, but never before one like that one."

With a final pat he headed for the Ace High and much-needed food.

When Slade entered the Ace High, Dirk Hudson was standing at the end of the bar. He nodded cordially and waved a greeting.

Well, Slade reflected grimly as he ordered everything in sight, if Hudson had been the tall masked man who ordered him pegged beside an anthill, he was certainly a past master at controlling his emotions. He looked not the least surprised or perturbed. Of course, someone might have seen him ride in the night before and relayed the information to Hudson, giving the saloonkeeper a chance to prepare against his appearance. That could be the answer, if Hudson really had taken a part in his capture and the subsequent ordeal he was forced to undergo.

As Slade waited for the food to be prepared, Hudson sauntered over to the table and favored him with a searching glance.

"What happened, get mixed up with a beehive?" he asked. "Your eyes are nearly swollen shut."

"Sort of," Slade admitted. "I collected a few stings."

"And I suppose one of the critters gnawed holes in your wrists, eh?" Hudson remarked dryly. "I've got something in the back room that will be good for you."

He departed, to return a few minutes later with a small jar of colorless paste with which he insisted on treating Slade's injuries, his touch deft and gentle as a woman's.

"The Indians were no snides when it came to concocting poultices and the like," he observed as he screwed the lid back on the jar. "Mom taught me how to make this, of herbs and berries, and I've never encountered its equal as a soothing and healing ointment; you'll notice a difference in half an hour. Here, take it along with you, just in case you get stung someplace else."

With a grin he sauntered back to the bar.

Slade took his time over his breakfast and before he had finished eating he did notice a difference. So much so, in fact, that when he left the saloon he immediately repaired to his room and smeared the ointment on the other numerous hives and welts with which his body was covered, making sundry remarks appropriate to the occasion as he did so.

To tell the truth he was utterly baffled by Hudson's conduct. And he was developing an uneasy feeling that he was completely off the track in suspecting the saloonkeeper. But if not Hudson, who? He didn't have the answer.

His next visit was to the doctor's office on the chance that Cole had returned to town. He had.

"Arn's definitely on the mend and there was no sense in me hanging around any longer, so I came back to town this morning," he said. "What the devil happened to you?"

"Got stung by some ants," Slade replied with perfect truth. Doc looked a bit incredulous but did not comment.

"Sime's over to the Ace High and wants to see you," he observed.

Slade got the impression that the physician was not turning loose all there was to be said and he wasted no time hunting up Bowman. The impression was not lessened by the queer look on the rancher's face as he gestured to a vacant chair.

Slade drew up the chair and sat down. He accepted the drink Sime ordered and glanced at him curiously.

"Well?" he asked.

"Well, Doc figures Arn will pull through, all right, thanks to you," Bowman replied. "He woke up late last night and 'peared a lot better than I'd hoped for."

Bowman seemed to hesitate, eyeing his companion.

"Did he have anything to say about what happened?" Slade prompted.

Sime Bowman hesitated again. "Yes, he had something to say," he replied slowly.

"What?"

"I asked him if he knew who shot him," Bowman answered. "He said yes, he did, that the hellion stepped out of the brush just before he pulled trigger. He said, 'Sime, it was Cocha. It was Cocha just as Dad described him many a time, war bonnet and everything.' I told him he must be loco, but I couldn't shake him. He kept repeating, 'It was Cocha, just as Dad always said he looked. It was Cocha.' Doc saw he was getting excited and made me stop questioned him. After a while he went to sleep again, but the last thing he said, drowsy-like, was, 'It was Cocha!' Slade, what the devil does it mean? Do the dead come back to life again?"

"I don't think so," Slade replied quietly. "I hold that Arn just made a mistake. One Indian looks a lot like another, to a white man's eyes."

"Not a six-foot, blue-eyed Indian like Cocha," Bowman declared positively. "His Spanish blood showed strong—he wasn't any darker than you."

"But, Sime," Slade said. "If Cocha was alive now he'd be an old man and would show his age. He wouldn't look like he did when your father knew him."

"I reckon that's right," Bowman conceded. "But the way Arn described him was the way he looked when—when he—died—"

Bowman's voice trailed off and he sat gazing stonily in front of him. Slade stared at him incredulously.

"Good Lord!" he exploded. "You're not trying to tell me that *you're* beginning to believe Cocha's ghost is riding the hills!"

"I—I don't know," Bowman answered. "It's all so crazy and mixed up. I—I don't know what to think."

Slade drew a deep breath. Sime Bowman gave every appearance of being an eminently practical individual, the sort one would expect to be totally free from superstition of any kind. But there was no doubt but that he was badly shaken and uncertain in his own mind.

"One thing is sure," Sime observed, "you'll never be able to convince Arn it wasn't old Sun Man who shot him."

"Sun man?"

"Yep. That's what we used to call him. Cocha's Apache name was Man Under the Sun. That's what the Mexicans always called him. Rather, they shortened it to Under the Sun. Never referred to him by anything else."

" 'Man Under the Sun!' " Slade repeated. Thoroughly familiar with the language of Mexico, the Spanish translation dinned in his ears like a thunderclap. "Under the Sun! Bajo El Sol! Bajo El Sol!"

Abruptly everything was crystal clear, the mystery of Cocha's "ghost" no longer a mystery.

For moments Slade sat appalled at what he had learned,

trying to properly evaluate and coordinate it with what had gone before.

He reviewed incidents that hitherto had appeared to have no significance, loose ends that were beginning to tie up. Now there was a plausible explanation of the seemingly senseless attacks on the Bowmans and the equally senseless, on the surface, efforts to stir up trouble between the Bowmans and their neighbors. And it was fairly obvious how the outlaw band operating in the section was able to obtain information supposed to be in the possession of but a select few.

He debated telling Sime Bowman, but decided not to, for the present, at least. He had to admit that of the moment he had absolutely nothing definite on the man in question, no proof of wrong doing on his part. Besides, although he did not believe so, he might be making the same colossal mistake he had made relative to Dirk Hudson. It would be better to remain silent until he could back up any accusation he might make.

"You didn't ride in alone today?" he asked Bowman.

Sime shook his head. "And not likely to after what happened to Arn," he answered. "I've got five of the boys with me. They're up at the Blue Wolf."

"And ride in the middle of them," Slade advised. "Don't get ahead or lag behind."

"You figure I'm still in danger?" Bowman asked curiously.

"You are," Slade replied flatly.

Bowman shook his head and sighed. "Beginning to almost wish I'd never come to the darn section," he grumbled.

"I've a notion that sooner or later you'd have been in danger anywhere," Slade answered. "Very likely coming here was the best move you could have made."

Bowman gazed at him in puzzled fashion, but Slade did not see fit to elaborate.

"How'd you cut your wrist?" Sime asked. "It's all swole up."

"Bridle strap got wrapped around it and gave it a wrench," Slade replied, again with truth. Sime chuckled.

"Thought maybe you'd got in a wring with somebody," he commented. "Your face looks sort of puffy around the eyes."

"Nope, didn't get into a wring," Slade disclaimed, and deftly changed the subject.

"I sent word to Sheriff Cross what happened," Sime said.

"He rode up and said he'd investigate. Reckon that's about all poor old Jess can do, investigate. Sol Bajo showed up while he was there. He said he was getting very much in the notion of pulling out of the section, with nobody safe the way things are going."

"I wouldn't be surprised if he does," Slade remarked dryly. Bowman nodded and finished his drink.

"Reckon I'd better amble up to the Blue Wolf and corral the boys and head home," he announced. "Don't want to leave Arn too long. I figured I should ride in and tell you about what he said."

"I'm very glad you did," Slade answered.

Bowman lumbered out, but Slade sat on at the table, smoking and thinking. Grimly he admitted that he had been wrong and the old Mexican *pastor* had been right. The spirit of Cocha *was* riding Bone Canyon and the hills, seeking to consummate an oath of vengeance sworn fifteen years before. Yes, Cocha's spirit still rode, but not as a shadowy ghost in graveyard panoply.

For a man's spirit lives on in the persons of his children. Over the great war chief's grave, young Cocha had sworn an oath, had sworn to be avenged on his father's killer. But Captain Lije Bowman, who split old Cocha's skull with his sabre, died before young Cocha could wreak his vengeance on him. Naturally with the vindictiveness of a people who continue a blood feud from generation to generation, young Cocha's hate transferred to the sons of the cavalry captain. And young Cocha, though more white than red, had inherited two outstanding Apache traits: the ability to effectually conceal his emotions under any circumstance, and patience. He could wait for his hate. Through the years he had waited, until Fate or whatever inscrutable Power that guides the hand of Fate provided opportunity. When the sons of Captain Bowman took up residence in the Bone Canyon country, young Cocha felt the time was ripe for the execution of his vengeance, and he had been endeavoring with all his power to execute it on the persons of Sime and Arn Bowman. And more than once he had very nearly succeeded. Only the wit, courage and sound judgment of El Halcon, Texas Ranger, had thwarted him so far.

And while stoically awaiting an opportunity to vicariously even the score, Cocha had operated as an outlaw in

the section, and with no little success. Slade recalled that
for several years a small outfit of Apaches and a few rene-
gade whites had raided in southern Arizona and New
Mexico and the lower Big Bend country of Texas. There
was little doubt but that young Cocha, supposed to be dead
but in reality very much alive, was the head of the compact
and skillful band that had continually eluded capture.

Why did he endeavor to foment trouble between the Bowmans and the Harlows? The answer was obvious; it provided a perfect cover-up for him. When the Bowmans were
found murdered, there were plenty who would attribute
their killing to the Harlows. Even those who espoused the
Harlows' cause would to a certain extent be beset by doubts
and no exhaustive investigation would have been launched.
And bumbling old Wes Harlow had done all he could to
play into young Cocha's hands. If the attempt to drygulch Sime Harlow in the mouth of Bone Canyon, right
after young Arn had had a run-in with the Harlows, had
been successful, the conclusion that the Harlows were responsible would have inevitably been arrived at. Only Slade's
presence had saved Sime Bowman, and his swift and ac-
curate appraisal of the situation had convinced him that the
Harlows could not possibly have engineered the drygulching
attempt, causing him to practically eliminate the Harlows
as suspects so far as the attacks on the Bowmans were concerned.

Bajo El Sol! There the cunning devil had slipped a little,
thanks to Slade's knowledge of Spanish. Ancestral names
are sacred to the Apache, and he is loath to part with the
one bestowed upon him. Young Cocha, although he was in
blood three-quarters white, was steeped in the traditions of
the Apache and by training and association *was* an Apache.
But with a white man's reasoning, he realized, when he decided to escape from the reservation, that he must change
his name. So the two strains of blood had compromised. In
deference to tradition, he had worked out a name that
would not altogether part with his identity as an Apache
and the son of the great war chief. The result—Sol Bajo!
A passing comment. There was little of the Apache in his
physical appearance, less so even than in the case of his
father. He had no trouble getting by as a white. Slade had
to admire his ingenuity in the alteration of his name. It

was perfect. And had it not been for the chance remark dropped by Sime Bowman relative to the translation of old Cocha's Apache name. Slade was forced to admit he would very likely never have caught on to the subterfuge. It had been pretty generally conceded that young Cocha was one of the victims of the Cripple Creek massacre in the Animas Valley. So Slade could hardly censure himself for not having considered the vengeance angle and the oath sworn by Cochas' son.

He couldn't help admiring the callous hellion's shrewdness and the adroit fashion in which he had conducted his campaign. His small horse ranch, manned by four punchers, all local residents of good repute, lent him an aura of respectability. And with plenty of leisure, it was not remarkable that he chose to augment his income by working for Dirk Hudson in spare time. He had wormed himself completely into Hudson's confidence. And Hudson was a friend and associate of Bill Higgins who, as a bank director, was conversant with the institution's plans to handle gold and money shipments. Higgins had confided in Hudson and Bajo had no difficulty getting information from Hudson.

So the mystery was nicely cleared up, so far as Slade was concerned.

Fine! But what the devil was he going to do about it? His mission was to break up the outlaw bunch infesting the Bone Canyon country and bring the evil-doers to justice. And, incidentally, to try and save the lives of Sime and Arn Bowman. So far he had been fairly successful at doing that, but the other chore was something else. He could denounce Sol Bajo as Cocha, a run-away Indian—and he might have difficulty proving it. To what end? If he proved his contention all he could hope for was to have Bajo sent back to the Arizona reservation. He had not one iota of proof that Bajo was responsible for the depredations committed. As an Indian, Bajo would be a ward of the Government and the Government would defend him against charges brought against him. And a smart Government lawyer would make him, Slade, look like a fool. In anything but a complacent frame of mind, Slade left the saloon and took a walk in the open air.

He could always think better in the open, but this time the sunshine and the gentle breeze did not seem to help much. His body still burned and itched somewhat, so he repaired to his room and another treatment with Dirk Hudson's ointment. It was all the saloonkeeper claimed and, feeling much better physically, at least, he drew a chair to the window and sat smoking and gazing out at the deepening twilight.

The soft twilight gave place to full dark. Overhead the bonfire stars of Texas burned in a blue-black sky and seemed to brush the mountain crests with their silvery flame. Pearson's busy night life began to hum. Slade went out and took another walk, vainly wrestling with the problem that confronted him, seeking a solution and finding none. He paused at the Ace High, which was already well crowded.

"Don't see anything of Bajo," he remarked to Dirk Hudson as they had a drink together at the bar.

"Hasn't been in for a couple of days and isn't coming in tonight," the saloonkeeper replied. "Been pretty busy at his place of late, I guess. His boys are here, though, all four of them. Sol sold a big herd of horses at a good price, nearly all he owned, and he said the boys had earned a bonus and a bit of relaxation; so he sent 'em in town for the night. He treats his hands well."

Slade nodded, and wondered uneasily if Bajo was up to some fresh devilment. Maybe he was planning to pull out. His good-bye to Slade pegged by the anthill had hinted as much. But Slade recalled that he had also intimated that he still had business to attend to in the section before leaving.

Just what was that business? Certainly nothing so innocent as the disposal of his stock and other property.

Slade's thoughts turned to Sime Bowman. He wondered, did the rancher get home all right? Surely, with five of his men riding guard over him. But just the same his uneasiness increased. He strongly suspected that the "business" Bajo had mentioned had to do with the Bowmans. Did he plan a raid on the Lazy B ranchhouse? Seemed ridiculous to even think of. There were a dozen men in the Bowman bunkhouse; and, Slade was pretty well convinced, Bajo had only two of his small band left. Four had been killed in the course of the attempted robbery of the stage and it was doubtful if the bunch ever numbered more than half a dozen.

But his uneasiness persisted, and with it a feeling that all was not well with the Bowmans. Finally he gave up. He got the rig on Shadow and headed for the Lazy B ranchhouse at a fast pace.

When Slade reached the Lazy B headquarters he saw that the bunkhouse, set more than a hundred yards from the main building, was dark; but a light burned in the living room of the ranchhouse. Dropping the reins to the ground, he dismounted and knocked on the front door. There was no response. He waited a moment, then turned the knob, found the door was unlocked and pushed it open.

A scene of ominous quiet met his gaze. The room was deserted and the glow of a lamp seemed to accentuate the sense of loneliness. And near the center table lay an overturned chair.

18

SLADE stared at the chair; it had a sinister look, so out of place in the orderly room. As he hesitated as to what his next move should be, he heard a feeble voice calling from the upper floor. He hurried up the stairs, saw a door leading to a lighted room standing ajar. He opened it and entered.

Younk Arn sat propped up in bed. He was pale and wan-looking but his eyes were bright, his expression animated.

"Why, hello!" he exclaimed. "Where'd you come from?"

Slade ignored the question and asked one of his own. "Where's Sime?"

"Darned if I know," Arn replied. "He was downstairs a while ago. I was drowsing and I thought I heard him talking to somebody, and something like a chair falling over. But when I roused up a bit and decided I wanted some fresh water I couldn't get any answer. Reckon he must have slipped out somewhere for a minute."

"I think I know where he is," Slade replied soothingly. "I'll take care of the water and then go fetch him. Meanwhile I'll have one of the boys from the bunkhouse sit downstairs till we get back; you shouldn't be alone in the house.' '

He procured the water from the kitchen, placed it within Arn's reach.

"Be seeing you soon," he said and walked down the stairs in leisurely fashion. Once outside he burst into dynamic action. He raced to the bunkhouse and knocked preemptorily.

"Come in," called a sleepy voice. "Who is it?"

Slade entered and announced himself, "I want one of you boys to go up to the house and stay with Arn," he told the occupants of the darkened room. "Sime's been called away for a little while. Be seeing you when we get back."

"Okay," the voice answered, "I'll be up there in a jiffy."

Slade left the bunkhouse, mounted Shadow and rode to the

123

trail. There he hesitated. It was not hard to surmise what had happened. Bajo, whom Sime had no reason that he knew of to fear, had been admitted to the house. He had doubtless managed to knock out Sime and had carried him off. Slade bitterly reproached himself for not following his first impulse to warn Bowman against Bajo. Well, it was too late to do anything about that now. The big question was, where had he taken the rancher? To that infernal anthill out on the desert? Not beyond the realm of possibility. Then Slade abruptly recalled that Bajo had sent all four of his hands to town, ostensibly to celebrate a bit. Really, the chances were, to get them out of the way for the night. Yes, Bajo's ranchhouse was his best bet. He headed Shadow north at top speed.

And he knew well that once again the great black was running a grim race with death.

Shadow seemed to know it, too, he spurned the earth with flying hoofs and the miles rolled steadily behind. In an incredibly short time Bajo's ranchhouse came into view.

Slade drew rein some distance from the house. He led Shadow away from the trial and covered the remaining distance on foot. The front of the house was dark but a light burned in the rear. Slade softly turned a corner, approached a glowing window and, keeping back in the shadow, peered through, and went rigid with horror.

The room, evidently the kitchen, was brightly lighted by two lamps. Standing to one side, their dark faces expressionless, were the two stolid Apaches who had pegged him by the anthill. In the middle of the room stood Sime Bowman, naked. His arms were stretched above his head, his wrists lashed to rings set in a ceiling beam. His ankles were secured to similar rings in the floor. His face was contorted with agony, his chest and legs streaming blood from a multitude of shallow cuts that laid open the flesh in a grisly pattern.

Standing in front of him, wielding a blood-stained knife, was Sol Bajo, on his countenance an awful look of hate and triumph. Even as Slade stared, the knife flicked out gracefully and a red furrow ran from hip to ankle. Bowman writhed in his bonds and a low moan escaped his lips.

Slade reached for a gun; but he dared not shoot from the angle at which he stood lest he kill Bowman. He glided back from the window, looked frantically about. Just beyond the window was a door. Slade hit it with his shoulder, all his two hundred pounds of bone and muscle behind the frenzied lunge. The door flew open with a crash and he was in the room.

The Apaches gutteraled startled yelps and went for their guns. Slade shot right and left, again and again. They went down, kicking and clawing in their death agonies. Sol Bajo whirled around, his face contorted with rage. His voice rose in the wild Apache war whoop, his hand jerked back and the long blade buzzed across the room like a streak of light, ripped through Slade's left arm and caused him to drop one gun. With the other he fired pointblank at Bajo.

Bajo reeled back, screamed again and hurled himself straight at the muzzle of Slade's flaming gun. Heedless of the slugs that battered his body, he closed with the Ranger. Slade pulled trigger again but the hammer clicked on an exploded shell. He flailed at Bajo's head with the empty gun, Bajo dodged and Slade's arm came down across his shoulder with numbing force. The gun flew from his hand and Bajo's fingers, like talons of steel, coiled about his throat. Slade tore at his corded wrists but was unable to free himself from the dying man's grip of maniacal strength. Red flashes stormed before his eyes, his breath choked in his constricted throat.

They carromed into a table, sending it crashing in splinters to the floor. Chairs went to matchwood under their feet. Slade battered at Bajo's madman face, but Bajo, blood pouring from his mouth and the gaping wounds in his breast, held on. Sime Bowman lunged, twisted in his bonds, moaning and cursing, but unable to free himself.

His face black with suffocation, his brain reeling, Slade gripped Bajo's wrists once more and whirled himself around and around, lifting Bajo's feet clear of the floor. With a final mighty effort that took every ounce of his failing strength, he tore the clutching fingers from his throat and hurled Bajo across the room.

Bajo's body thudded against the wall and slid to the floor in a bloody heap. Slade, breathing in great gulps, staggered across the room and knelt by the dying man, in his steady eyes a look almost of compassion. Bajo strained to raise his clutching hands and could not. Slade spoke thickly, the words laboring from his aching throat, "Trail's end, Cocha! The end of the vengeance trail! A bad trail to ride, Cocha—the vengeance trail!"

Bajo arched his body from the floor, tried once more to lift his hands, choked on the blood in his throat and fell back, dead.

Slade straightened up, stumbled to where Sime Bowman sagged in his bonds. With trembling fingers he fumbled a knife from his pocket and cut the rancher down. Bowman lurched off balance but Slade caught him before he fell and eased him into a chair.

"I ain't hurt bad," Bowman mumbled. "He didn't cut deep."

With a shaking hand he gestured to a heap of black grains on a small table that still remained standing.

"Powder!" he gulped. "After he finished with the knife he was going to stuff it in my mouth and set it off; would have blown my face to pieces. He was a devil!"

"Yes, in the light of things as we view them," Slade replied. "But the Red Man's ways are not the White Man's ways, we must consider that. An eye for an eye and a tooth for a tooth is his code. Well, you'll find that in the Old Testament of our own Bible. Maybe right now he and his father are talking things over in the Happy Hunting Grounds, where there is no hate and no vengeance. I hope so."

"Bajo's great ambition, of course," he continued, "was to torture you and Arn to death, thus consummating the rite of torment and the oath of vengeance in true Apache tradition; but once again his White blood compromised with the Red. He would have been at least partially satisfied to just kill you and Arn, or have you killed by the Harlows. He was daring and utterly ruthless. Witness his attempt to rob the Alhambra cafe. And right up until the very last his luck stayed with him. Dirk Hudson had to go and pick just the time Bajo went through a window to get his face cut by flying glass and start me thinking seriously on Hudson. But his luck ran out in the end, as I've noticed it usually does for folks who ride a crooked trail."

"Stay put, now," he added, "and I'll try and patch you up a bit."

He went to the door and whistled Shadow. When the horse cantered to him he took a roll of bandage and a small jar of antiseptic ointment from his saddle pouches and treated Bowman's wounds as best he could.

"You're bleeding yourself," Sime commented. "Did he knife you?"

"Blade nicked my upper arm," Slade replied. "Here, wrap this handkerchief around it and it will be okay."

With Slade's aid, Bowman got into his clothes, wincing and swearing the while, for it was a painful process.

"What happened at the house?" Slade asked.

"Bajo came in," Bowman replied. "I didn't think nothing of it, of course; thought he'd just come to inquire about Arn. Reckon when my back was turned one of his darned Apaches slipped up behind me and belted me one. Next thing I knew I was roped to a horse. They brought me here and trussed me up. Then Bajo told me he was Cocha's son and went to work on me. Feller, you sure have a habit of happening around at just the right time; I thought I was a goner. How the devil do you do it?"

"Just luck, I reckon," Slade smiled. "Well, guess the time for cover-up is over, seeing as I'll have to explain things to the sheriff. Didn't do much good anyhow; the ones I didn't want to spot me were on to me all the time."

He slipped his Ranger badge from its secret pocket and pinned it to his shirt. Bowman stared at the famous star.

"So that's what you are!" he marveled. "Well, I'd ought to have known it. Nobody but a Texas Ranger could do the things you do."

"Yes, I'm a Ranger," Slade answered. "Captain McNelty sent me here to investigate the trouble. I ran into rather more than I bargained for. Well, think you can ride? Arn is liable to get worried about you if you don't show up at the house soon."

"I'm okay," Sime said, standing up. "I'm darned glad to be able to ride, walk or crawl. Let's go!"

With a last glance around at the scene of death, they left the ranchhouse. They found four horses, saddled and bridled, tied to the corral bars. The saddle pouches were stuffed with staple provisions and a very large sum of money. Appeared that Bajo and his braves had planned to pull out after the son of Cocha wreaked his vengeance on Bowman.

"You can ride one and we'll take the others with us and turn them over to the sheriff when he shows up," Slade decided. "Except that money is part of the Gonzales payroll robbery. You can send one of the boys to fetch Cross from Cooper."

Sheriff Cross arrived early the following morning. He gazed at the star on Slade's breast and shook his head.

"And Wes Harlow wanted me to make you a deputy!" he grunted. "Wouldn't be such a bad notion, at that. And Sol Bajo was old Cocha's son! Well, I guess you laid the ghosts, and I hope nobody raises up some more. They're too darn active."

Slade and Bowman rode with the sheriff when he headed for the Bajo ranchhouse, the latter having decided he'd better pay Doc Cole a visit and get patched up a bit more.

They dropped in at the Alhambra later. Some of the Lazy B punchers had already spread the story of the night before's stirring happenings. Old Wes Harlow was there, shaking his head and swearing. Slade steered Sime Bowman to his table.

"You two shorthorns have had a little lesson of what happens when decent folks get to rowing among themselves and leave things wide open for owlhoots to move in," he told the sheepish-looking pair. "Now I think you'd better stop pawing sod and get together."

Old Wes lumbered to his feet. "Reckon it's up to me to take the first bite of crow, Bowman," he said. "Suppose we just forget everything that's happened and start all over. And here's my hand on it."

Slade smiled down at them, his cold eyes all kindness. "That's better," he applauded. "Figure I can leave you with an easy mind. Yes, I've got to be riding. Captain Jim will have another little chore lined up for me, the chances are, by the time I get back to the Post. *Adios!*"

They watched him ride away, tall and graceful atop his great black horse, to where duty, danger and new adventure waited.

THE END

www.ingramcontent.com/pod-product-compliance
Lightning Source LLC
Chambersburg PA
CBHW020147180626
46810CB00004B/1765